TO STAND IN THE BREACH

TO STAND IN THE BREACH

DANIELLE GRANDINETTI

HEARTH SPOT PRESS

H S P

PRAISE FOR *TO STAND IN THE BREACH*

"Inheritance battles, labor strikes, and a sweet Irish romance to root for... *To Stand in the Breach* is the Depression-era tale you won't want to end."

- KELSEY GIETL,
author of *Broken Lines.*

"A page-turner, *To Stand in the Breach* combines suspense and romance that leads the reader through a thoroughly engrossing tale of what it means to stand with those you love."

- ANN ELIZABETH FRYER,
author of *Of Needles and Haystacks*

To my sister,
whose love of horses inspired Clover's tale

And I sought for a man among them, that should make up the hedge, and stand in the gap before me for the land, that I should not destroy it: but I found none.

 EZEKIEL 22:30

But let all those that put their trust in thee rejoice: let them ever shout for joy, because thou defendest them: let them also that love thy name be joyful in thee.

For thou, Lord, wilt bless the righteous; with favour wilt thou compass him as with a shield.

PSALM 5:11-12

CHAPTER 1

Monday, February 13, 1933

He found her.

Desperately clutching the paper, Dr. Katy Wells slipped into the sheltered area between two of the buildings at the center of the small town of Eagle, Wisconsin. She placed a gloved hand on the worn plank wall of Town Hall and squeezed her eyes shut to block out the words on the letter. Fear's insidious claws sank into her chest. Fourteen years of running, of staying one step ahead of her uncle and other men who wished her harm ... and she'd finally found security here, in this town, hidden as it was in the middle of the United States.

Until today.

Farmers she knew from her veterinary rounds passed along the walk in front of the buildings, coats closed against the chilly wind despite the bright sunlight. None of the men glanced her way. Still, she stepped deeper into the shadows. She couldn't face any of them. They only knew her as a competent large-animal doctor, someone who—apparently, miraculously—saved countless creatures these farmers thought past help. Not a one would guess her a girl given to fits of panic.

She tried to iron the wrinkles out of the letter with a trembling hand. It came from the matron at the boardinghouse where she had lived while studying veterinary medicine at Cornell. The matron had written what she obviously considered good news based on her cheery tone. Katy's family had been searching for her—of course they had, as Katy had vanished fourteen years ago ... on purpose. They had tracked her to Ithaca, New York. Now, they were on a train to Wisconsin, if the matron was to be believed.

Och, why had she opened the letter before the farmers' meeting? She needed every ounce of her courage to stand up in front of all those men. If only that New York newspaper hadn't published an article on the handful of female veterinarians who had graduated from Cornell in the last couple decades. The reporter focused on the first woman in America, who had received her Doctorate of Veterinary Medicine just twenty-three years ago, but mentioned other graduates as well. Graduates like Katy. That must be the way her uncle had tracked her to Wisconsin.

She pushed from the wall, carefully folding the letter before tucking it into her medical bag. Then she smoothed the gray fabric of her skirt, as if that action could smooth her troubled heart. She needed to put the letter, her uncle, and her past out of her mind. This afternoon's meeting was not about her. In fact, knowing these farmers as she did, they likely wouldn't appreciate her interrupting their meeting. Normally, she'd happily leave them to their own devices. She'd rather face down an ornery bull than walk the gauntlet of men inside.

But this meeting affected her patients, which meant she needed to speak up.

Chin held high, she stepped into Town Hall and allowed her eyes to adjust to the dark interior before entering the assembly room. Angry shouts blurred with the rushing in her ears. Animals she could manage. This?

Eagle's Town Hall comfortably held the collection of dairy farmers, but Katy couldn't drag in a deep breath. She pinned her eyes on the American flag that hung behind the podium. The symbol of freedom laughed at her. Even an ocean hadn't hidden her from Uncle Patrick. *Put it out of your mind.*

Step by step, she made her way down the center aisle. *For my patients*, she told herself, *for the cows*. Two-thirds of the way toward the front, men began turning their attention on her. Whispers stung her ears. She could guess what they were saying, what they were thinking.

They might trust her to save their ill horse or deliver a breech calf, but when it came to business, she wasn't welcome. If not for the cows …

"Dr. Wells?" The sound of her name snapped her eyes from the flag to the man behind the podium. Mayor Rolland. "What are you doing here?"

She squared her shoulders against the accusation in the man's voice. "I'm here to speak for me patients."

Deep, male laughter rippled through the room, raising the hair on Katy's neck. She hated being a lone female, and it didn't help that nerves deepened her accent. Sweat dripped down her back. She tightened her grip on her medical bag, which held emergency medical supplies and a few personal items. It promised the security of her profession.

"We know our cows, missy." A man beside her leaned close enough for her to smell the tobacco chew tucked into his cheek. Farmer Wallace. He owned her least-favorite farm to pay house calls to. He might have a wife and nine kids, but he had a wandering eye that made her distinctly uncomfortable.

"I reckon you do, but she's the doc." Joey Moore, her dearest friend's twin brother, gave her a subtle wink as he stepped out of the crowd, looking as dashing as ever in his black suit, his policeman's badge shining on his shoulder. "If Doc Holland gave his medical advice, we'd listen to him. Why not extend the same respect to our animals' doctor?"

"Stay out of this, copper." Mr. Wallace spit tobacco juice at Katy's feet. "You left your pa's farm, so you ain't got no say."

"He's right, Officer Moore." Mayor Rolland tapped a gavel on the podium. "You're here to keep the peace, so keep your opinions to yourself."

Joey inclined his head and moved closer to Katy. His presence solidified her courage. Ever since his twin, Lily, had met Katy at an animal husbandry class several years ago, Katy had felt welcomed into the Moore family. She felt a kinship with Lily, who left her family's dairy farm to train hunting dogs. Her late grandfather willed her the house she lived in and the property where she conducted her business. In fact, it was the same grandfather who got Katy set up as a veterinarian here in Eagle, too. He'd reminded her so much of her own grandfather that, for the first time since escaping Ireland, she'd felt as though she'd finally found safety.

"My son is right—Dr. Wells is my veterinarian." Joey's father crossed his arms as he stepped into view. Overalls hung on his thin frame. "I want to hear what she has to say."

Joey gave her a nudge and Katy ascended the platform. Mayor Rolland did not give up his podium, so Katy stood to the side, silently rehearsing her speech as she waited for silence. The farmers, who paid her in coin and produce, who called her when their knowledge of animal care was expended, gathered before her. She was a veterinarian. University trained. She could do this.

"I'm not here to be influencing you for or against striking." Katy wrapped and unwrapped her fingers around the handle of her medical bag as she got directly to the point. "As you said, the business of dairy farming is not my area of expertise. The cows, however, are what I know. I'm here to make sure that if you decide to strike, you'll still be caring for the cows and the calves about to be born."

"What do you take us for?" Mr. Wallace spit another stream of tobacco juice, sending a jolt of disconcerting apprehension up her spine. "Half the cows are dry, and we aim to dump the rest of the milk. We ain't giving it over for such a low price."

"He has a point, Dr. Wells." Mr. Moore spoke with more civility than Mr. Wallace, even if he seemed to agree with the man. "The current price of milk is pure thievery—almost half of what we were getting just a few years ago. That's why we must join with the Wisconsin Cooperative Milk Pool in an organized strike."

"And the cows?" Katy willed her voice not to quiver. "You will continue to amply feed them? Keep watch over the cows ready to drop a calf? Care for their udders to avoid infection? They mustn't grow ill over this."

"If we don't make enough money and this drought continues, worrying about whether the cows are being properly cared for will be the least of your worries, Dr. Wells." Mr. Moore leveled stern eyes at her.

"Hear, hear." Mr. Wallace pounded his fist in his hand. "Them calves may not have a farm to belong to if we don't dump the milk."

"You're really all right wasting good milk?" Appalled, Katy stared at Mr. Moore, then scanned the room. "When so many are going hungry and your dairy products could feed them?"

"Our families are hungry, too," said another farmer, Mr. Broader, sounding more sad than angry.

Mr. Moore clapped the man on the shoulder. "Exactly. It's the leanest time of year. It costs more to bring the milk to market than dump it on the side of the road."

"Why should them processing plant owners like Booth get rich off our backs?" Mr. Wallace adjusted his trousers." The government ain't doing nothing, so we have to."

Other farmers agreed.

"That's good enough, now." Mayor Rolland banged his gavel. "The government is doing all it can. And I think you have done enough, Miss Wells. We do not need to get off topic."

Off topic? To the medical issues cows and calves could face if not properly cared for during the strike or the starving thousands throughout the United States? Mayor Rolland gave her a pointed stare, and she swallowed down the words begging to escape.

"Come with me, Dr. Wells." Joey reached to help her down from the platform.

She allowed him to assist her, numb and confused over the reaction to concerns. She had expected to be unwelcome, but to be summarily dismissed?

Joey pressed his hand against the small of her back, directing her through the crowd to the blessed freedom of the outdoors. She inhaled the cold, February air, letting it calm her from the inside out.

"Thank you." Katy gave a weak smile. As nice as Joey usually was to her, she needed distance from the male species right now. Especially a handsome one, even if he was her dearest friend's brother.

"Dr. Wells, wait." Joey snagged her arm. Startled, she yanked away, and Joey held up his hands as if in surrender. "I'm sorry you weren't welcomed in there. You know how it is, right? The farmers know their business."

"And I know cows."

"So do they."

Katy pursed her lips to keep from spouting just what she thought of such an arrogant statement. It wasn't until relatively recently that men deigned to even milk cows, and now they were the experts? Ha!

"May I escort you back to your truck?" Joey drew down his eyebrows. Was he concerned or angry? She'd believed her perceptions of men before to her detriment, and with the way her day had gone so far, she felt no inclination to trust one right now.

Weariness weighted her limbs. Worry over her patients, worry over the matron's letter, worry over what she should do. Hollyhocks ... she simply wanted to be alone.

"Katy?" The concern in his voice brought out her more genuine smile.

"I'll be fine." Katy patted his arm. "You can get back inside."

He covered her fingers with a callused hand, the action melting a bit of her carefully built wall of protection. Fear jolted her into action. Without an explanation, she practically ran down the sidewalk. Just as she'd run from Ireland, from England, from New York. Now she might have to run from Eagle too.

Joey rubbed his neck as he watched Katy sprint away from him. She'd always been shy, quiet—the very reason he'd been intrigued the first day his sister Lily brought her to family dinner. Over time, he'd come to appreciate how her expressions betrayed the deep well within. If only he could grasp the mystery behind her protective façade. But she was his sister's friend. He didn't dare act on his curiosity, or his twin would rain down fire—especially if her friend got hurt.

Opposite personalities, Katy and Lil. One reserved, the other blatantly independent, yet both preferred their work with animals over humans and neither seemed interested in getting married, as much as he'd like to see his sister safely settled. He'd tried to tease Katy's story from Lily, but she was notoriously tight-lipped about confidences.

He huffed out a breath as Katy's truck drove out of town. Every time he debated her effect on him, he came to the same conclusion—it was too risky to pursue her. And now, more than ever, he couldn't let himself get distracted, not with this strike business. A small local police force meant his chief needed every man at his best. Nope. He wouldn't let Katy get in his head.

The farmers were in an uproar when Joey returned inside the meeting hall. Men shouted over one another from both sides of the center aisle. Mayor Rolland banged his gavel on the podium to no avail. Joey couldn't even make out what the farmers were arguing about. He put two fingers between his lips and let out a shrill whistle. It sliced through the air and cut off the noise.

"Mayor?" Joey gestured toward him. "Your floor, sir."

The pudgy mayor banged his gavel twice more. "It's time to put this debate to a vote. You all know I am against the strike proposal. It will hurt our town in a time when resources are already too tight."

"Which is why we need to strike," Dad called out from the front row. "If we don't get Booth and the other dairy processing plants to raise what they pay for our milk, we'll be put out of business. And taking away profits is the only way to be heard."

"At the expense of your farm?" Red infused the mayor's jowls.

"A temporary inconvenience for future gain." When Dad paused, Joey held his breath. His father's next statement would be a dart aimed directly at the mayor. "Unless the *government* finally *does* something about the prices."

Joey closed his eyes, dropping his chin to his chest as the mayor slammed the gavel against the podium. Why did his dad always have to go for the jugular in arguments like this? It alienated people who did not already agree with him. His supporters, however, rallied behind Dad as if he were a figurehead. Perhaps owning the largest and most prosperous dairy farm in the county gave him that position naturally, but to go up against Mayor Rolland didn't seem like the smartest plan. Wouldn't peace and calm negotiation be wiser?

Whatever the case, the time for talk had passed. The mayor called for a vote—to strike or not to strike. Joey hoped with everything in him that they opted not to strike. Strikes turned violent, and as an officer of the law, he dreaded being put in the middle of a physical alternation.

CHAPTER 2

Tuesday, February 14

K aty stoked the fire in her woodstove, then set the coffee pot to boil. Her hands hadn't stopped shaking after she reread the matron's letter this morning after chores. A cup of her strongest brew should settle her nerves. *Daideó*, her grandfather, made the perfect cup of coffee. Dark, strong, and thick. It coated the stomach as it did the heart. Hers came a distant second, but it'd do the job.

She hadn't slept much last night, torn between duty and fear. As much as she preferred escaping before her uncle found her, she couldn't just desert her patients—not with calving season beginning in earnest any day now and the possibility of a milk strike bearing down on them. Which meant she needed to come up with an alternate plan for when her uncle showed up on her back step.

As she poured coffee into her cup, one name floated up with the steam. Dare she trust a man? Her experience said only grandfathers were reliable, but Joey Moore wasn't just any man. He was Lily's twin brother, and Katy trusted Lily. Surely, she could trust Joey too.

Not something she could decide now. This morning, she would give her attention to her patients. First, she needed to visit the Broaders' farm to check on the cow that had been showing signs of pregnancy distress. Then, despite every desire not to, she had to visit the Wallaces' farm. One of their draft horses had gotten snagged on barbed wire two days ago, and yesterday morning, the gash began festering. She also needed to visit the Andersons' farm to treat a cow's sore she had to lance yesterday. Hopefully it would look better today.

After finishing her coffee, she donned a white blouse, then fastened a divided skirt around her waist before adding a fitted jacket to give her a functional yet proper appearance. Hiking through mucky fields and animal barns made it difficult to maintain decorum, let alone keep her clothing clean, but she was determined to display a professionalism that would outshine her gender. Especially with farmers like Irvin Wallace.

She split her black hair into two braids that she intertwined into a bun at the back of her head, then pinned her hat in place. Respectable, plain, and all business. Medical bag in hand, she made swift work of locking up her house, but as she turned to her truck, she found Joey Moore leaning against it, ankles crossed, arms folded, and a frown giving him a deadly serious expression.

Katy stumbled to a halt, her heart pounding in time with the questions swirling in her head. Joey squinted. Katy backed up a step. Joey's frown softened, and he lowered his arms as he pushed off the truck. Katy scolded herself for her reaction. It was Joey Moore, not Mr. Wallace.

"I came to tell you they voted to strike," he said as he neared.

Katy switched her bag to her left hand. "They'll be dumping the milk?"

"According to my dad, for the next five days, they plan to withhold their milk unless they get the price they want for it."

"Withhold?"

Joey folded his arms again. "They hope the pressure of withholding supply will force the price of milk higher."

"You do not look happy."

"I'm not." He frowned again. "It's a foolish plan that won't work. There are too many farmers who need the money and who won't buy into this strike. And if Eagle's mayor won't press for better prices, what's the likelihood other mayors will? If the state's mayors won't listen, it's doubtful the governor will pay attention, which means prices won't change."

Katy ignored the anger wrapped up in Joey's words. "What will they be doing with the milk if they do not sell it?"

"Dump it, turn it into butter—I don't know."

"They won't be changin' their cows' diets to make less milk, will they?" Katy adjusted her grip on her medical bag. "Or changin' the milking schedules? It be calving season, and any change in diet could harm the cows and calves."

"I don't think they have a plan, which is why I'm here." Joey lowered his arms just to put his hands on his belt. "The farmers who wish to strike are going to be distracted. They're going to be lined up on the road."

"And not on their farms."

"Exactly. Which potentially means not having anyone watching the cows who could be calving."

"They would risk them comin' to harm?" Katy matched Joey's expression.

"My dad would say if the price of milk doesn't go up, they'll have to sell the cattle, anyway."

"Och, how did it get to this?"

Joey gave a humorless laugh. "You don't really want to know."

Katy shrugged. "And you'd be right—I don't. I do not care about politics, about opinions, or grandstanding. I do care about my patients. If those cows have no one to advocate for them, I will."

"You do know they're just cows, Dr. Wells."

"Just cows? Hollyhocks, Joey Moore. They are animals God created. And if that is not enough, they provide sustenance and material benefit to thousands of people. Even these cows have worth."

Red crept up from Joey's collar. "I'm not denying they have worth, Dr. Wells."

Katy waved her hand as if she could wipe away Joey's embarrassment. "I'm only meanin' that where most people see cows as property, I see them as living beings. That may simply be a byproduct of bein' their doctor, but they matter to me."

"No wonder you and my sister are friends."

At mention of Lily, the tension left Katy's shoulders. Yes, that shared view of an animal's worth was just one of many reasons why Lily Moore had managed to convince Katy to join her in Eagle. And another reason why she was loath to leave. She doubted she could replace a female friend who shared her philosophy on animals.

"Dr. Wells?" Joey dragged his toe in the dirt before tentatively meeting her eyes. "Are you busy this evening?"

"Busy?" Tension inched back.

"Would you do me the honor of going for a walk with me after supper?"

Joey wanted to call on her? "Why?"

"Because, I—because it's Valentine's Day."

"Joey." She laid a hand on his forearm and lowered her voice as if to keep her words secret from the birds overhead. "There be a myriad of girls who would love your attention on such a romantic holiday."

"You're not wrong."

But Joey didn't seem happy with the truth of that statement. Maybe this was the opening she needed to tell him about the matron's letter. Yet she couldn't send mixed messages. She wasn't interested in a relationship, in marriage. Not now, not ever.

"What about tomorrow?" Katy pulled back, and Joey distinctly felt the absence of her touch.

"I can't." He shoved down hurt at her rejection same as he shoved his hands in his pockets.

This had been a dumb idea hatched over a cold cup of coffee in his lonely apartment across from the police station in town. He'd meant only to deliver news of the strike. All right, not entirely, not if he was honest with himself. The lure of the holiday was too much not to use the strike as a reason to see the pretty veterinarian. Against his better judgment.

She had a point—most girls fell over themselves to say yes if he asked them, which is why he didn't. He hated the claustrophobic feeling of expectation, especially from females. Katy, though? She kept him at arm's length, which is what intrigued him. And stung. What was he thinking, taking the risk and asking her out? He should have simply assuaged his desire to see her and kept his mouth shut.

"With the strike, it's all hands to keep the peace." He shrugged.

Compassion filled Katy's blue eyes. He'd always been struck by the dichotomy of her looks—the dark hair and complexion paired with the brilliantly bright blue eyes and equally bright smile, when she chose to show it.

"Right." She gave a rather business-like nod. "You best be coming tonight, then."

"Wait. What?"

Katy withdrew even further, fiddling with her medical bag. "I'm needin' to ask you something, but not now. I need to see to me patients."

His antenna rose. This wasn't about a date, but it was the most she'd opened up to him since they met. No way would he squander the opportunity. "Is everything all right?"

"Come tonight, and we will take that walk." She avoided eye contact and made haste to her truck. Her dark dress caused her to blend in with the deadness of winter, as if she did everything in her power not to stand out. The prickle of unease sharpened against his neck.

"Katy, wait."

She paused, hand on the door of her truck. She didn't look back at him.

"Do you need me to come with you?"

She opened the door without acknowledging him.

Horsefeathers. "Do you *want* me to come with you?"

She slid into the driver's seat, but he caught the glimmer of a smile as she glanced at him. "I'll be seeing you tonight, Joey Moore."

Stubborn woman. Joey rubbed his jaw to hide his own smile and lifted a hand in goodbye.

"Right, and how be Clover today?" Katy set her doctor bag on the edge of the horse stall and held her hand out to Clover's nose.

Mr. Wallace leaned on his pitchfork, chewing a wad of tobacco. "He ain't eating much more than yesterday and ain't letting me near his leg."

"Let's take a look." Katy ran her hand up the gelding's white forelock, then around his neck before reaching for the latch to open the stall. "Easy boy. We be keepin' it slow."

"Just open the d—" Mr. Wallace reached for the halter he'd already secured on the horse. Clover jolted away from him.

"He be a mite skittish, Mr. Wallace." Katy kept her tone calm to soothe both horse and man. "Might'n you spare a carrot from the cellar?"

The man ground his teeth for a moment, then slapped his leg. "I'll ask the missus."

"Thank you, Mr. Wallace," Katy called after him. She rested her cheek against Clover's. "Now that it's just us, how about we look at that leg, eh, boy?"

Clover nosed her.

Talking the whole time, she led Clover out of his stall and secured him in the main aisle of the barn. Ropes tied to his halter held him steady between two posts. Katy ran her hands over the horse's dark coat, getting him used to her touch, her smell, her presence.

Clover was a draft horse, a Percheron, Katy guessed, with his muscled neck, broad chest, and relatively stocky legs and back. By no means a small animal, Clover stood almost seventeen hands high, meaning Katy's head didn't even come to his shoulder. But the large beast had a heart of gold—of that, she was sure.

"Easy now, boy." Katy eased her hands toward Clover's left leg. "I'll just be taking a quick look."

Clover sidestepped into Katy, and Katy scooted her feet out of the way of the horse's massive hooves.

"*Tsk, tsk.* Never pleasant to have a wound probed."

Clover wagged his head, ears back.

"See, now? We agree." Katy pressed her right shoulder into Clover's left side, leaning over to get the horse to give her a hoof, just as a farrier did when he shod a horse. Clover reluctantly picked up his foot, and Katy tucked it at an angle where she could see the upper part of the leg between the horse's elbow and knee. Carefully, she peeled away the dressing.

Hollyhocks, the wound looked angry. Clover kicked his injured leg out of Katy's hands.

"Not good news." Mr. Wallace spit a stream of tobacco juice into the hay littered on the barn floor, an odd look in his eye making Katy keep close to Clover.

"Right, and I need to clean it out again." Katy attempted to sooth the agitated horse. "While I visit another patient, gather a couple neighbors who can hold him down. I plan to return midday."

Mr. Wallace tossed the carrot on the ground at Clover's feet. "I ain't needin' no more of your services."

The hairs on Katy's neck rose. "Pardon?"

"I ain't needing no more of those services." Mr. Wallace leered.

Katy returned to the bag, gathering the supplies she needed to re-bandage the leg.

"I say, you ain't needed here unless—"

"I need to bandage the wound." She cut off his proposition, something she'd taken to just ignoring every other time she paid a call to his farm. He'd yet to physically act on it, and she knew how to keep an animal between them.

"Well, I need a healthy horse, one that works my fields."

Merciful heavens. Was he seriously considering putting down his horse? "Mr. Wallace, once the wound be properly clean, Clover will be back on his feet in a matter of days."

Mr. Wallace spit another stream of tobacco juice. "I've already talked to the bank. I'm buying a tractor and ain't keeping a sick horse that I can't sell."

Getting kicked in the stomach would hurt less than the emotionless declaration of his intent to end an animal's life. Sure, he'd been left with an impossible choice between caring for a loyal but injured animal and the good of his farm. But to have no sorrow over the decision?

She shivered. "I'll buy Clover."

"What?" He stared at her, and Katy fought the urge to hide behind the horse.

"I'll buy him, subtracting any medical costs he's incurred since the injury." Katy named a price that would leave her with little even for the groceries she would need by the end of the week. It was less than Clover was worth, but considering the circumstances, maybe it would be enough to save the gelding's life. She'd worry about the details later—like how to feed both Clover and herself.

A calculating gleam lit the farmer's eye. "You have yourself a deal."

CHAPTER 3

Joey parked in the dark, just out of sight of Katy's place, and ran his hands over his cleanly shaven jaw. Was he really doing this? Really calling on Katy Wells? His twin's closest friend and the woman who often joined his crazy family for Sunday dinner?

Of course he was, because at each of those meals, he found himself attentive to every word she spoke—and there weren't many of them. It only made him more interested in finding out who the real Katy happened to be. Setting his shoulders, he put his Model A into gear and pulled into her yard. He wouldn't stay long. The chilly conditions would not permit a lengthy walk, and he wouldn't cause her discomfort by inviting himself into her house, especially at this time of night.

A gust of wind threatened to kick his hat from his head as he walked to her back door. He jammed it down more securely. A knock brought no answer. His nerves tangled in his already knotted stomach as he knocked again. Had she forgotten? Did an emergency arise? Her truck was here. He circled the house, finding no light coming through the windows.

Maybe the rumor he'd heard in town was true.

He spun on his heel and headed for her barn. Through the cracked-open door, he spotted a lantern at the same time the sound of her singing reached him.

"*Oh, Danny Boy, oh Danny Boy, I love you so ...*" The haunting melody had him pausing in the barn's doorway to watch her as she brushed a dark horse—Wallace's draft horse, just as he'd heard.

She still wore the same plain clothes from this morning, matching the animal as if she sought to disappear against him, her hair so dark it blended with the shadows cast from the lamp. The thought that she wished to hide caused an ache to well within. Or maybe it was the song?

"... *but when ye come, and all the flowers are dying, If I am dead*— Och! Joey Wells, you be scaring me silly, standing there like a spirit!" Her accent strung her words together, as if they were a musical instrument.

Joey shook such a strange idea out of his head but couldn't dislodge the haunting sadness the song left behind. He looked around the barn for something to inspire a clear-headed thought. A dairy cow stuck her head over the stall door to his left. The next stall's door was lower, allowing a donkey to stare at him with black eyes. He'd forgotten Katy used a donkey instead of a horse for her plowing and carting needs.

She cast him a shy smile.

He blurted the first thing that came to mind. "Don't think I've heard that song before." He could still hear the melody in his head.

She patted the horse's shoulder, and he noticed a bandage stretching from the top of the horse's leg down to its hocks. "It's popular amongst us Irish. Reminds us of home."

"Do you miss it? Ireland?"

She bustled about, setting her grooming tools in a wood box that rested on a small table along the wall opposite the stalls. The movement effectively hid her expression from him. Hiding again. Did she wish to keep her emotion or something else from him?

"Katy?" He stuffed one hand in a trouser pocket.

"Most times, no. I certainly have no desire to return. My life is … here." Her voice cracked on that last word. She turned to the horse and in that instant, he caught a glimpse at what she'd been hiding. Yes, emotion, but it wasn't nostalgia. It was pain and maybe even fear. Pain and fear meant danger. He eased his shoulders back, slowly worked his eyes over the barn, and tuned his ears to any noise outside.

"A cow took most of my attention before getting back to the Wallace farm. Then I needed to tend Clover's wound before bringing him home. More debris got inside the cut, and it was festering something fierce. Should be better now." She barely paused for air. "The Broaders paid me in supper, and it's more food than I can eat meself. Come to the house, and I'll share it with ya—cornbread and a delicious-smelling stew."

She appeared hopeful, but Joey shook his head. "It's barely proper for me to be in here alone with you. Let's take the walk we talked about this morning."

Tears watered her eyes.

He felt like a heel. "Katy, I'm sorry, I—"

Clover nudged her shoulder, and she laughed, sliding a finger beneath wet eyelashes. "Do not apologize, Joey Moore. You are a rare, good man, if that be your answer to my foolish invitation. I should not have asked."

"Then why are you … crying?"

She took a shuddering breath. "Help me put Clover in his stall, and I'll be telling ya as we walk."

Katy tucked her gloved hand in the warm crook of Joey's arm as they strolled along the dirt road that passed in front of her house. The clear sky above allowed the moon to light their way. The nippy air sharpened her senses. Her cheeks simultaneously warmed with Joey's proximity and stung with the cold. The smell of decomposed foliage blended with manure, a distinctly rural blend she found oddly comforting since it reminded her more of Ireland than the filthy streets and tenements of London or New York City.

"I'm not so good at waiting for answers." Joey tugged at his collar. "Want to go easy on me and tell me now?"

Katy chuckled. "Right, I'll be telling ya. Goin' easy on ya, now, that be up for debate."

"Shouldn't have said that, huh?" The smile he gave her made her stomach flip.

"Likely not. But I'll be merciful." Hollyhocks, was she flirting with him? Right before telling him *this* story?

He frowned, all teasing gone. "That serious?"

"I s'pose it is, at that." She cringed at the strength of her accent and determined to tamp it down. She hated Joey thinking of her as a needy foreigner rather than his twin's friend requesting his help.

Joey stopped them and turned to face her. "Katy, are you in trouble? In danger? You can tell me what's wrong."

His intensity had Katy taking a step back.

Joey rubbed his neck. "I want to help. What can I do?"

Could she really tell him? She hadn't even told Lily. Or anyone, for that matter. With trembling fingers, she pulled the folded letter out of her coat pocket. Ever since Lily brought Katy to her family's home, she'd been impressed by how Joey treated his mother and sisters. He didn't talk down to them. In fact, he seemed overly protective of them. She knew it drove Lily crazy at times, but Katy had often felt distinctly jealous of it.

That feeling of longing gave her the courage to hand over the letter. As Joey read it, a puzzled expression bloomed across his face, the moon highlighting him like a searchlight. She had no doubt her story would bring out a strong emotion in him. Katy hugged herself, hoping against hope that Joey would offer security, not disgust. Whichever emotion he chose would show her the truth about his character. *Dear God, please let it be the one I've seen him exhibit before.*

"Isn't it good that your family found you?" Joey handed the letter back to her.

Katy shook her head as she folded the paper and tucked it away. This was it. She met his gaze. No judgment. Yet. "Have you heard of the Magdalene Laundries in Ireland?"

"You were a laundress?"

Oh, she couldn't do this.

He touched her shoulder, a gentle touch. "Tell me."

Katy tucked her hand back in Joey's arm, needing the security as she explained. "It is an asylum for women. Unmarried women who ... Och, this be rather uncomfortable."

"It's all right. I think I follow. What does the laundry have to do with you?"

"I was born there."

Joey cringed. "Did you grow up there?"

Katy shook her head. "Sixteen years old, my mother was, but she wouldn't name my father, so the entire community insisted on sending her to the closest laundry to work out her sins. They didn't want her influence on the other young ladies in the village."

Joey's muscles tightened beneath her hand.

"Daideó, my grandfather, tried to stop them, to ask them to wait until the baby was born, but as a widowed father himself, with no wife to be the example for their wayward daughter, he was overridden. The one thing Daideó could do was rescue me from growing up in the laundry. My mother escaped long enough to smuggle me to Daideó and since he couldn't keep my mother free, he protected me as best he could an illegitimate girl."

"Until?"

"His funeral." She blinked against the tears and cleared her throat. "The very day Daideó was buried, I overhead my uncle making plans to send me to the laundry. I'll never forget overhearing him tell my aunt, but I could hardly believe it when she adamantly agreed."

"Why would they choose that for you?" The question held anger, confusion, and disbelief. That last scared Katy. "Because your mother was unwed?"

"Partially. Females who were seen as too beautiful were considered too dangerous of a temptation to men, especially with a background such as mine. Those women were sent to the laundries just like those caught in scandalous acts or anticipating a child without a husband. The goal of the laundries was to rehabilitate their waywardness."

"Because a woman was pretty?"

Katy nodded. It shouldn't sound as ludicrous as Joey made it out to seem. She'd fought against enough male expectation since leaving Ireland to make her wonder if her uncle should have sent her to the laundry. That maybe something was truly wrong with her—beyond being pretty—that led so many men to want her in a way she didn't welcome. But she'd also heard enough rumors to know the laundries were more like a workhouse or a prison, especially since Daideó couldn't even rescue his own daughter before it cost *Máthair* her life.

"That's why you wear the clothes you do, isn't it?" The quiet question pulled Katy from the dark reverie.

She nodded again. Her clothing was her armor. It helped in some cases, yet it barely fended off men like Mr. Wallace. So if word got around about her past, even her choice of dress wouldn't help.

Joey led them along a field, dormant from the winter, the ground partially furrowed and frozen in clumps. Soon the farmer would turn it over—prepare it for spring planting. Last year, it had corn. No, wheat. She couldn't remember.

"How did you get away? From your uncle?"

"After Daideó's funeral, while the townspeople still gathered, I simply slipped away. Put me most precious possessions in a knapsack and ran toward the coast. I never sensed any pursuit, so I suspect they didn't realize I'd left until too late to follow me trail. They probably felt relief not to have to worry about me anymore."

Joey made an odd noise.

Katy forged on. "I stowed away on a boat headed for England and made me way to London. I didn't feel safe at any of the farms along the way—a girl on her own, ya know—so I kept going till I could disappear in a right big mass of people. Eventually, I found an Irishwoman who gave me lodging in exchange for cooking and cleaning. About three years later, somehow, my uncle found me."

"What happened?"

"I went to the sea again. Attempted to slip aboard a boat bound across the ocean but was nearly caught. An Irish family told the officials I was their daughters' nurse. They got me to America, and I stayed with them in New York City. The husband died two years later, and the wife remarried." Katy's stomach churned at the memory of that second man's attempts to lay a hand on her. "Let's just say, I stayed away from her second husband until I could save enough to escape to Cornell."

"Wait." Joey stopped in the middle of her yard. "That all happened before you went to the university? How old were you when your grandfather died?"

"Twelve."

Joey's jaw dropped, then tightened. "Your uncle thought a twelve-year-old girl needed to be rehabilitated because she was pretty? That's ..." A cheek muscle twitched. "And this uncle, he's coming here?"

"Right. It appears so. Usually, I run away. But this time, I don't want to leave Eagle. My animals, my patients, my friends ..." She stared up at him, willing to drop to her knees and plead outright if it made any difference, but the concern she saw in his face held her upright. "Joey, how can I stay?"

He snatched up her hands. "I'm a police officer, Katy. I won't let your uncle harm you."

Praise you, God. "I hoped you might feel that way."

The pressure of his grip tightened, but not in a threatening way—rather, in a way that conveyed strength and security. Now she could only pray his protection would be enough so she wouldn't lose everything.

CHAPTER 4

February, 15, 1933

The unusually brisk wind at his back and the pleasantly warm sun on his face, Joey tried to focus on the growing crowd of farmers blocking the road to Booth's Dairy Processing Plant the first morning of the strike. Most were farmers he'd known his whole life. Old farmers whose fathers or grandfathers had fought in the war that divided the country. Only a few who'd participated in the more recent Great War since that generation provided the food to feed both soldiers and home front. And young farmers, like his brothers, who were building their homes with wives and hope for a better future.

However, Katy Wells never strayed far from his mind, his thoughts tangled over her story and the protection she would need if her uncle showed up. Legally, he didn't know what her uncle could do. Katy was a grown woman, after all. Yet someone who threatened to send a woman to an asylum simply for being beautiful—what type of trouble would he make for her here? Why not simply let her go, especially after so long?

That question bothered him the most.

"They're peaceful enough." The voice came from behind Joey, startling him into nearly pulling his gun.

"Andy." Joey released the burst of adrenaline in a breath. "Don't sneak up on me like that."

A teasing glint lit the man's eye as he rested his forearms on the four-foot-tall brick wall that surrounded his family's processing plant. Blonde hair flopped over his forehead.

"Stow it," Joey warned, crossing his arms and leaning his backside against the wall. He and Andy had gone to school together but weren't friends—never had been, in great part, because of their fathers. He had little use for a conversation with the man, but Andy's appearance here probably didn't lack a purpose.

"You know Dad's not going to bend, right?" Andy squinted at the farmers, yet lacking the sun-wrinkled creases of every man before him. None of them seemed to notice him, which was good, because who knew what fracas they'd raise over his presence.

"My dad won't either. Not when the people from the Wisconsin Cooperative Milk Pool are behind this." He glanced at Andy, gauging his reaction as he added the threat of the other large cooperative joining the fight. "It'd be worse if the Farmers' Holiday Association decided to get involved."

"They still might if we can't solve this in the next five days."

We? Joey raised his brows. *Huh.* Maybe the man did understand that a coordinated strike backed by not one, but two of the largest dairy farmer cooperatives could spell disaster for everyone. Or finally prompt the powers that be to fix the problem. One never knew until the crucible hit. He studied the man beside him, perhaps there was more to him than that gray stripe suit. "You've got something in mind?"

"Maybe." That tone. He recognized it from their school days.

"I won't like it, will I?"

"It involves your sister."

"Lily?"

"Uh, no. Amy."

Joey's younger sister? He studied the man beside him. He supposed he could grudgingly admit Andy appeared to have matured over the past few years, considering the lack of joviality on his face. Still. "What about her?"

Andy rubbed a hand over his jaw. "I should have asked before all this started, but with market struggles, I thought it better to wait until I had firmer footing. Seeing the farmers and what they're willing to do for their families, it got me thinking that waiting isn't the right thing to do. I know it's unconventional for a younger sister to marry before her older one, but …"

"Spit it out, Booth."

"I came to you first because you're more level-headed than your dad."

"You're testing that theory." Joey moved his hands to his hips, closer to his revolver. "Get to the point."

"I want to ask Amy if she'd let me call on her."

"I got that part. Why?"

"I like her."

"What does any of this have to do with the strike?"

"I need a way to convince your dad to let me see Amy. If Amy is not interested, I won't even try. But if she is, maybe she and I can bridge the gap. A peace treaty, of sorts. At least here in Eagle, we could have a fighting chance of this strike ending well, for everyone."

Maybe the man really had matured on the inside too. He didn't even flinch at Joey's scrutiny. "You really care for my sister? This isn't a ploy?"

"I'll make you a deal, Joey. You ask her first. If she's not interested, I won't ask at all. If she is, I'll wait until after the five days scheduled for the strike to talk to your dad. Maybe our dads can work things out before then so I don't need to leverage the strike."

"Doubtful that'll happen." Joey rubbed his neck.

"I agree. And we can't depend on the government fixing things. President Roosevelt wants another two months to enact his hundred day new deal ideas, but what can he do all the way in Washington to help farmers here in Wisconsin except force processing plants like ours to pay more for milk?"

Joey raised an eyebrow. "Raising the price of milk is good for the farmers."

"I'm not denying that." Andy straightened and turned, mirroring Joey's posture, but with his back to the farms. "Raising prices is not good for the processing plants—and before you argue—those extra costs would move down the line. To the consumers."

"The people who are out of work and can't pay for it, anyway."

"Exactly." Andy sighed.

"Then what's the point of striking?" Joey's head spun just thinking about it.

"Because the farmers aren't making a profit, either, which means they can't feed their families."

Joey tapped his thumb on his belt, hiding his growing respect for his old classmate. "And if the weather stays dry like it has the past few years, the crops will continue to fail, which means not enough feed. Hungry cows don't produce, so there will be less milk to send to the processing plants. We're in trouble if something doesn't change."

Andy met his eyes. "That's why we have to work things out here at the local level before things get worse for the farmers and businesses in our community. We can't depend on getting rain any more than we can wait for impersonal people to make decisions for us. Did you hear the governor's response to the strike? He's saying he'll give the farmers a chance to fix things with more committees and legislature."

"So there's hope this strike won't end in violence?"

"Unlikely if we leave it to theory and words and never *do* something to change the situation. That's why, if Amy agrees, perhaps we can pro-actively work to bring about a mutually beneficial conclusion for the people of Eagle."

With that passion, the man should run for mayor. Joey scanned the crowd before returning his attention to Andy. "I'm all for finding a solution that benefits everyone, but I always thought marriages should be built on love."

Andy shrugged. "Times like these, maybe we just don't have that luxury. That said, I do care about your sister. A lot. I promise you that."

"If you're willing to walk the line between your dad and ours, maybe you really do." Joey sighed. "I can't promise anything, but … I'll talk to Amy."

Andy grinned.

Marriages should be built on love. The words echoed in Joey's head throughout the rest of the day. Many of the farmers gathered had daughters who attempted to finagle a reason for Joey to call on them—nice girls for whom he had no strong feelings, whereas his twin had definite ideas on marriage. Ideas the townspeople disagreed with, that Joey disagreed with. She was too independent for his way of thinking. Did Katy feel the same as Lily? She also lived independently. Somehow, her reasons for living alone felt different than why Lily insisted on living at their grandfather's old place.

As he reached his apartment across from the station, Joey wished he could check on Katy. This late at night, it wouldn't be proper, so tomorrow he'd try to get away from the strike line earlier. His instinct said she needed protection. His protection.

Did Amy need it, too, or was Andy's interest true? If they got together, would it be enough to bridge the milk divide? Was it fair to ask that of her? Today the farmers hadn't caused any trouble, but he had the distinct impression their anger merely simmered below the surface. They simply weren't desperate enough. Yet.

And his own father might be the one to ignite the slumbering volcano.

Cold night air slipped through the cracked-open barn door as Katy groomed Clover, using quick, circular strokes with the curry brush, the action fitting her mood. All night, she'd fought the feeling of being unable to breathe and, while it was chilly out, she needed the extra air movement. She leaned into the large horse, who stood like a stalwart statute, his tail and skin twitching slightly as Katy hummed.

If she thought hard enough, she could pull up a mental image of Daideó's cart horse. Smaller than Clover and speckled white, he had the same calm temperament as Clover. Katy loved the memories of riding in the cart beside Daideó as he went on his veterinary rounds and of his gentle laugh as he told her story after story from years working among animals. Having Clover made Daideó feel that much closer.

She set the curry comb aside and chose the hoof pick, needing to give her arm a break from working over such a large animal. Tapping Clover's leg, she instructed him to lift his front right foot. Resting the massive hoof on her own knee, she meticulously cleaned out the grass, pebbles, and debris caught in the sole. As she released Clover's hoof, she ran her hands from fetlock to the forearm, checking the tendons. All appeared healthy. She repeated the actions on Clover's back two legs before moving to the front left, the one with the injury. Clover sidestepped as Katy reached for the foot.

"Easy, boy," Katy soothed. "I need to check the bandage."

Slowly, she peeled away the cloth, revealing the slash from the barbed wire.

"Ah, this looks much better." The angry festering had turned to a healing red color. It would still take time and care to keep the wound healing properly, but this turn meant Clover was on the mend.

From the grapevine, she'd heard Mr. Wallace had already sold his other draft horses and purchased a John Deere Tractor. A risky move for both farmer and bank. Perhaps the sale of the horses had brought in enough money to reduce the risk. She hoped so for the family's sake. She would hate to see the Wallace children go hungry.

Katy collected materials to re-bandage the wound. Clover nickered, one of his ears angled forward, the other back, and he pawed the ground with his injured leg.

"What is it, me boy?" Katy paused to listen, catching the sound of a car.

Glenn, her donkey, and Nessa, her small dairy cow, both stilled in their stalls. Glenn's ears went straight up. Katy's heart beat in her ears. Darkness was falling, so perhaps the strike had ended for the day and Joey had decided to stop by? She shook her head. Why would he do that? If trouble came, she would need to find him. Or leave Eagle.

Glenn grew more vocal, Clover tugged on his harness ties. Katy left her medical supplies on the table and edged toward the barn door. She didn't recognize the car—and she knew most of the vehicles in Eagle, seeing as how she visited every farm at some point or another. A tall man climbed her back porch step. From here, she couldn't make out any features. The darkness would soon be complete enough, she wouldn't be able to see him at all.

Did she stay here or go out to meet him? He didn't seem in a hurry, so no animals could be in immediate danger and in need of her medical knowledge. He wore a suit, so not likely a farmer. Most importantly, he didn't look anything like she remembered of her uncle and was definitely not as old.

He knocked at her back door, then stuck a hand in his trouser pocket as he scanned the yard. Katy stepped into the shadows so he wouldn't notice her. Oh but he would notice the lantern light if he looked this way. And there, he turned.

Indecision froze her as he walked toward the barn. It was not a large building in which to hide. Five stalls on the right, two of which were empty, her tack and equipment rooms on the left, and the hayloft above. Hay she needed to stretch between three animals now, one of which ate seemingly more than the other two combined.

The horrid panic she kept carefully concealed narrowed her vision, but she shoved it away. She couldn't hide. She needed to face this head on. It could be someone new in town or someone following up on her speech at the town hall yesterday. She wouldn't know until she asked.

She pulled the barn door open wider so the man knew he could enter but didn't issue a verbal invitation. Instead, she retreated to Clover's side. The big horse's ears twitched, his tail raised. She tucked herself beside his shoulder so she could lean into him. Glenn kicked at his stall, generally raising a ruckus behind her. He didn't like the strange visitor, and that didn't help Katy's turmoil or Nessa's agitation.

In another moment, the stranger slipped inside and closed the barn door all the way.

"May I help you?" Katy called, pleased her voice didn't betray her fear at this unconventional situation. She crossed her arms and raised her chin. If she put on a confident front, perhaps her mind would catch up.

"I am looking for Caitlin Wells." The Irish burr sent chills down Katy's back. She hadn't heard her home's accent since she fled New York, and this accent sounded as pure as hers had been when she first left Ireland. Had he come from Uncle Patrick?

Deep breath. "I'm Dr. Wells." She put on her professional demeanor and was infinitely grateful she hadn't changed out of her business attire after stopping by the Broader Farm to check on a cow nearing calving time.

"Fergus Cormac." He nodded to her and stepped fully into the lantern light. She did not know this man. Blond hair neatly trimmed. Clean-shaven face with angular lines. His thin stature filling out the narrow blue suit in a handsome way. But his blue eyes felt familiar.

"Mr. Cormac. What brings you by my farm tonight?" Katy forced every ounce of Irish from her voice.

He stuffed both hands in his pockets. "I'm a solicitor for the estate of the late Mr. Sean Wells. Your grandfather."

CHAPTER 5

Katy spun to her work table. Her fingers fumbled as she gathered the supplies to re-bandage Clover's leg. She needed to keep her hands busy as her mind raced over the implications of this lawyer's announcement. Was he the one who found her through her old boarding house matron? Perhaps it hadn't been Uncle Patrick as she thought. But as Daideó's solicitor, did he still have ties to Uncle Patrick?

When Katy turned around, Mr. Cormac had his hand held to Clover's nose, who backed away even as he stretched his neck forward to be sure the man didn't have a treat. Katy felt similarly. Anxious, yet curious.

"That's Clover," Katy offered. Glenn had stopped kicking, but based on the gray ears twitching over the stall door, he hadn't stopped keeping watch. "She be recoverin' from a run-in with a bit of barbed wire." Hollyhocks, her accent slipped out worse than ever.

"Your horse?" Mr. Cormac retreated, giving both her and Clover space. Nessa, whose stall was closest to the barn door—and now, Mr. Cormac—mooed at his presence. It felt as though her animals had her back, and it gave her courage.

"That he be." She ran her hand over Clover's shoulder as she approached, letting him know her presence. "Now, Mr. Cormac, you'll be tellin' me what brought you all the way from Ireland?"

His eyebrows shot up.

Katy hid a smile in her shoulder. "Not many Irishmen 'round these parts, and your accent is stronger than mine." She tapped Clover's injured leg, and the horse raised it for her to apply the bandage.

"I s'pose so."

"Daideó passed fourteen years ago." She glanced at him. "Pardon me, but you do not look old enough to be Daideó's solicitor. Why are you really here?"

Clover sidestepped, and Katy ran a calming hand over his shoulder before rapidly securing the bandage and straightening to meet Mr. Cormac's scrutinizing gaze. Only the sounds of Nessa's cud-chewing, Glenn's water-drinking, and Clover's snuffly huffs filled the quiet barn.

"Mr. Cormac?"

"You don't remember me?" Short blonde hair, nicely trimmed beard, lake blue eyes—like every other young Irishman in the town she'd grown up in.

Katy leaned into Clover's bulk. "We knew one another?" Why didn't she recognize his name, at the very least?

"Not exactly. Rather, I knew you, but I do not think you knew me." He rocked on his heels. "My father worked with your grandfather's solicitor, Mr. Murphy. I joined the firm after I finished university. As a lad, I would visit my father, and you would come in with your grandfather. He could be … absent-minded. Yet without fail, you, hardly older than a child, graciously handed him everything he needed. It made an impression on me in my youth."

Glenn rattled the water bucket in his stall. Clover pawed the ground. Katy frowned, sifting through memories of a past she had long since locked away. She hadn't thought anything of carrying paper and pencil and whatever else Daideó might have forgotten. His mind was always on the animals, a trait she admired. But that was over a decade ago, so why would a boy she couldn't even remember speak as though he knew her so well?

It didn't sit right. She met this solicitor as a businesswoman would, with directness. "You'll be telling me, Mr. Cormac—from the beginning, mind you—exactly why you are here."

"Shouldn't we go where it's more comfortable?" He gestured outside.

She wasn't leaving her barn.

Mr. Cormac sighed and moved to lean a shoulder against the outer wall of the tack room, far away from Nessa and Glenn. "You left home the day of your grandfather's funeral, correct?"

"In 1919."

"You never knew his last will and testament? Never heard it read?"

"I was twelve, Mr. Cormac. That was not the first thought going through me head." Especially after overhearing her uncle wished to put her into one of the laundries. She shuddered, and Clover swung his massive head toward her. She rubbed his velvety nose.

"Sean Wells was a good animal doctor."

Katy felt a blush rise as Mr. Cormac's expression said he recognized she had followed in her grandfather's footsteps.

"He also invested wisely. If you didn't hear his final wishes, then you don't know he died a wealthy man and left his entire estate to you."

"What be your meaning?" Katy tightened her grip on Clover's halter. The gelding snorted, prompting an echo from Glenn, and Katy let go, fisting her empty hand instead. "I mean, what do you mean?" Oh, she should stop talking before she appeared an imbecile.

The man gave an indulgent smile. "When you turned of age, you would have come into your inheritance. A goodly sum, mind you."

"Och, I can hear the *but* a mile off. Out with it."

"Your uncle wants the money." He paused, either for dramatic effect or to give her a chance to respond.

She didn't, as there was nothing to say to that tidbit. When didn't Uncle Patrick want money?

"That's why he wanted to put you into the asylum."

"You know about that?" Dread pooled in her stomach.

Mr. Cormac shed the relaxed demeanor and came as close as Clover would let him. Glenn brayed in his stall. "Your grandfather thought he had protected you against every contingency, even providing that if you were incarcerated or placed in an asylum, Mr. Murphy would manage your estate. The money would not be allowed to go to your uncle at all."

Oh, she didn't like where this was going. "Then why try to put me in that awful place?"

"Because the solicitor was in Patrick's pocket."

"Did Daideó know?"

"Think about it—he would have made other plans. As it was, it took them three years to find you in London. The uproar back home! When you did not come back with Mr. Murphy, everyone was convinced you were just like your mother. Not me, mind you. I knew you wouldn't have left without good reason. My only regret was not finding you sooner so I could help you. We were in London at the same time."

Discomfiture jabbed her chest like hens pecking corn.

"Seven years Patrick and Mr. Murphy waited," Mr. Cormac continued, seeming oblivious to her mounting panic. "Then they tried to declare you legally dead. I had just joined the firm and defied Mr. Murphy's orders to save your inheritance. We are similar in age, so I scoured the yearbooks of every university accepting female students on the continent and in America."

"You found me?" So many emotions bubbled inside, she was losing control of them.

"Just your name on Cornell's student list. It was proof enough you'd been alive within the seven years required." He grabbed her shoulders. "Don't you see what good news that was?"

Katy freed herself and swallowed. "T-that was four years ago. Why are you here now? Why not come then if you cared so much?"

"Because it was 1929." Mr. Cormac sighed as if releasing a great weight. "America was not the only place that experienced economic depression. I couldn't afford to come find you. And the past four years have been filled with many a hardship for our people. When the Fianna Fáil party came to power last year, it infused hope in the community, and Patrick renewed his effort to lay claim to your inheritance. My father insisted it wasn't in your best interest to be found, but Patrick would not let it go, and so my father and I dug into why. That's how we found out about the details of the estate. The last time I saw my father, he was headed to confront Patrick and Mr. Murphy. My father's body was found in a marsh a week later."

Bile rose in Katy's throat and she crossed her arms over her stomach to keep it from revolting. "I'm so sorry!"

"I came straight to America to find you. Caitlin, your uncle has a long memory, and that money has been sitting, untouched, for fourteen years. It's burning his soul. You must watch yourself."

She squeezed her trembling fingers into fists. "You think he'll come here?"

"Or send someone who will provide proof of death."

Cold washed over her. It simultaneously froze her fear and cleared her thinking. Could she believe Mr. Cormac's story, or was he the person her uncle had sent to kill her? She raised her chin. "W-what if I refuse to grant him the estate?"

"In case of your death, the money goes to the solicitor—Mr. Murphy—to be given to charity. With Murphy working with Patrick and my father out of the picture, I'm too junior a partner to be able to stop them from working around the law."

Katy scanned the barn, looking for an escape out the front door, or the rear, but she was sandwiched between Clover and Mr. Cormac. "W-what if I just give it to him? The money, that is."

Mr. Cormac advanced a step toward her like a panther stalking his prey. "You can try, but your uncle was willing to put an innocent, twelve-year-old girl in an asylum to get at that money, he was willing to have you declared dead, and he was also willing to kill my father. Do you really think simply giving him the money will satisfy him? He's a man to hold a grudge, Caitlin. He'll extract revenge whether he gets the money or not. I'm sure of it."

"Don't call me that." Katy squeezed her eyes closed and leaned into Clover. She hated her birth name. The name given to her by the nuns in the laundry that held her mother. Daideó had called her Caty, spelling it with a C, which she Americanized when she escaped from England. She refused to let this stranger call her a name she left behind.

"Whatever I call you won't matter to your uncle." Mr. Cormac's words were harshly spoken, but true.

She remembered her uncle well enough to know Fergus Cormac was exactly right. Patrick Wells had a long memory and an insatiable appetite for good living and good beer with a heavy hand he wielded without remorse. She needed to tell Joey these developments, but how could he help her now? She'd have to disappear. Again.

Would she ever be able to stop running?

"We could fake your death."

"What?" Katy stared at Mr. Cormac. Had she spoken aloud, and had she heard him right? "I don't want to do anything of the kind. Why would you suggest such a horrid idea?"

"Because if Patrick thinks you're dead, then you'll be free of him." The Irishman's bearing spoke of confidence and home as he leaned toward her.

But Fergus Cormac wasn't Joey Moore. "I might be free of my uncle as long as he never learns the truth, but what of my life here?" What would she do with Clover and Glenn and Nessa? How could she leave Lily and Joey? Or her calving patients caught in the midst of the strike?

"Is it not worth sacrificing what you have in order to be free?"

"I've done that already. Twice." She gulped at the air, leaning a hand on Clover's side, wishing Mr. Cormac hadn't closed the barn door.

"You have to do it one more time. It's the only way he won't find you."

The only way. Black edged her vision, but she blinked it back. "It's not that easy for an unmarried female."

"Then marry me."

Her jaw fell open.

"We'll run away together." Earnestness poured from Mr. Cormac's fair features. "I won't let Patrick touch you."

She shook her head, scrambling for a way to get him off this train of thought. She'd survived this long without resorting to a marriage of convenience, and she certainly wouldn't marry anyone with ties to her life in Ireland. "It won't happen, so you can dismiss that thought right now, Mr. Cormac."

"Why not?" He stalked closer.

Clover's muscles rippled under her hand. Neither of them trusted Mr. Cormac. He kept saying the right thing and yet not the right thing at all.

"Expecting company?" Mr. Cormac changed directions, moving to the barn door.

Horses hooves. Someone was here. Not Joey, or Lily—her heart sank before it lifted again—it was likely a farmer, which meant an animal needed her. She seized at the chance to escape and pushed past Mr. Cormac, who stayed out of sight in her barn.

"Dr. Wells?" The voice came from behind a lantern. The wagon creaked as a man leapt to the ground.

She hasted closer. "What is wrong, Mr. Broader?"

"It's one of my other cows." He yanked his dusty hat off his head. The Broaders lived on the same side of town she did, the one opposite the Moores' farm, which is why neither she nor the Broaders had electricity and the Moores did. Mr. Broader didn't have any motorized equipment, either, including a car. "She's having a rough time of it. I came as quick as I could."

She glanced back at her barn. What do to with Mr. Cormac? She feared returning with him inside, yet to reveal his presence could incite the very gossip that tormented her life in Ireland. In her line of work, animals depended on her to make life and death, split second decisions. She needed to make one now in order to save a cow and her calf.

"Wait here while I get my things. I'll follow you to your farm. When we get there, bring me boiling water and a pile of clean cloths."

"Thank you, Dr. Wells." His shoulders eased a bit from his ears. The man cared for his animals—she could tell that the first day she'd visited his farm and watched him instruct one of his five children how to care for an injured bird. Before Katy could inspect the sparrow nestled in the man's gloved hands, the stunned creature had stirred, and Mr. Broader had helped it fly away.

Doubt drained from her mind as she jogged to the barn. This was her life. She would not run. She would not marry a stranger. This time, she would stand her ground. She cared nothing for Daideó's supposed inheritance. He'd left her something far more valuable—her love of animals. And a mother and her baby needed her help right now.

Mr. Cormac stood at her table, studying her medical supplies. She had no more time for him and his wild ideas, but it helped to know Mr. Broader stood guard outside, even if the farmer was unaware of the fact.

"Nosey, are ya?" She shooed Mr. Cormac out of her way.

"Just interested."

"Right. A patient requires my assistance." She unhooked Clover and led him into his stall. "I need you to leave."

The pause as she settled the gelding seemed filled with only her pounding heart.

"Fine, then." Mr. Cormac studied her. "Think over what I've told ya, and I'll be in touch in a few days."

"I won't change me mind." She secured the stall door with more force than necessary. "I'm not leaving."

"Then be careful, Caitlin." Mr. Cormac grabbed her arm with a grip that had her gasping. "Especially until we can talk again."

CHAPTER 6

Fergus Cormac kept the car lights off as he followed Caitlin—Katy—Wells to a farm not far from her house. She met the same man who'd called her away, then followed him to a pasture near the barn. He could hear the cow's pained mooing from here. Dr. Wells left to do her job, not give him the slip.

That realization gave clarity to his plans. He'd been mostly honest with her about how he'd found her, the realities of the inheritance, Patrick Wells murdering Fergus' father. He didn't mention the real reason he hadn't come to America right away. Economic troubles wouldn't have stopped him. What had, was his mother. Or rather, her failing health.

Her death nine months ago refueled his desire to get to America as soon as possible. Then his father found an odd letter addressed to Mr. Murphy. The questions Fergus and his father dug up did indeed cost his father his life, so it was no hardship for Fergus to leave his parents buried side by side in the country they loved.

Fergus hesitated in the dark shadows. How could he leave Caitlin now that he'd found her after all these years? If only one of the ways he'd gotten to America had not been through agreeing to finish one of his father's outstanding cases. Fergus hadn't bothered with the details of it other than the fact a boy had been mistakenly sent to America as an orphan. Turned out, his nanny had kidnapped him but fell ill, and before his parents could locate him, he'd been sent away. Fergus' job was to bring him home. Simple, except Fergus wasn't leaving America without Caitlin.

If only she'd agreed to come with him tonight as he'd envisioned. Didn't she comprehend how much her care for her grandfather had impacted him as a lad? She was the kindest, most sincere female he'd ever met. Even more than his own mother, who treated his father like a king. How could this little town possibly appeal to her when she'd left Ireland behind? Or when he told her of her uncle's threats? Then offered her a way of escape.

Kindness. She obviously cared about her patients as much as she had her grandfather. If she needed time to think, to settle her affairs, the least Fergus could do was give that to her. He'd certainly bought her enough time, and he could be flexible, make adjustments, as he returned East to put that lost boy on the next ship home.

Resolved to this secondary plan, he turned his car toward Milwaukee and the train that would take him away from Caitlin Wells for the last time. Because when he returned to Eagle, he wasn't taking no for an answer.

CHAPTER 7

Wednesday, February 22

Five days passed at a gallop. Fifteen cows had needed her assistance. This last cow, she'd nearly lost the calf because the farmer took his precious time calling for her. He'd been on the strike line, and it took all her waning self-control to not say, *I warned you*. Not that this particular farmer would have listened. He only requested her help at the very last hope, leaving her no choice but to work a miracle to save her patient. Both of them.

Spent physically and emotionally, Katy parked her truck in her yard and headed straight to the pasture to see Clover, Glenn, and Nessa. Glenn waiting by the fence as she approached, the late-afternoon sun casting a golden shadow around him. Nessa merely raised her head, momentarily pausing her cud-chewing to acknowledge Katy, then she returned to her business. Her sides swelled with her unborn calf. Clover stood on the far side of the pasture, watching, ears twitching. When Katy unlatched the gate, the gelding came trotting over.

Katy gave equal attention to Glenn and Clover, petting their noses, scratching behind their ears, and rubbing their sides. Clover's wound was well on the mend now, but it left Katy with other questions. While Clover didn't favor the leg, other behaviors persisted that should have disappeared with the pain. Clover stuck by her side, his ears always moving, his tail always raised, and he never lay down in the grass, let alone rolled in the mud.

Her suspicions sat like a boulder in her stomach. Mr. Wallace's reputation and how quickly he was willing to end Clover's life gave substance to her thoughts, despite a disturbing lack of proof. Nevertheless, they firmed her resolve to keep Clover close, even if she couldn't afford it. If she accepted the inheritance Daideó left her, however …

"What do you say to a ride, Clover, boy? You've gotten so little exercise, and I think we both could use the fresh air."

Clover wagged his head.

Katy pressed her cheek against the horse's, then hurried to the tack room for a bridle.

She hadn't seen or heard from Mr. Cormac since he left her barn the other night, for which she was grateful. Other than affirming her wish to stay in Eagle and reiterating her adamant desire not to marry him, she had nothing else to say. Really, she could only wait for Uncle Patrick to drop the other shoe. It added to her weariness.

Her work saving baby calves over the past few days provided for the next several months since most farmers had paid her in hay for her animals or food for herself. With a cellar well-stocked with jams and preserves, an icebox with cream and butter, and a pantry with eggs and dried meat, she should feel content. However, once calving season was over, the surplus would end and worry would settle in once again.

Clover hung his head as Katy fitted the bit in his mouth.

"It's all right, me boy." She soothed him as she removed the blanket from his back. Clover didn't respond. He never did with a bit in his mouth.

Leading him through the gate, then along the fence, she climbed up onto his back. She didn't have the correct size of saddle for the large beast, so bareback would have to do for now. She didn't plan on going faster than a walk, anyway. Clover needed to ease into activity after such a quick cessation of labor. She directed him toward the back of her property.

The dormant ground made her yearn to prepare the soil for spring. To put down roots. Permanent roots. Now that she had a draft horse, maybe she could enlarge her fields. She and Glenn had only been able to cultivate a small portion of her land. Clover would be willing, but Katy doubted whether she would be up for such a task. Maintaining her garden and harvesting her small hay field took all her extra time as it was.

She needed a better plan.

Would Daideó's money be the answer? It would let her feed her animals and perhaps provide an excess she could use to help the poorer farmers, like the Broaders, so they needn't worry about compensating her for the care of their animals. Once things slowed down, she'd find a lawyer of her own to look into matters, if she could afford it. But money or no, it would do no good if her uncle found her. She needed a way to get him to leave her alone for good, and if it meant giving him the money, she'd figure out how to do that and still afford to keep Clover.

Then again, if he held the grudge she suspected he did, giving him the money wouldn't be enough. Only her complete humiliation would suffice. Katy shuddered. She worked hard to maintain the reputation she had in Eagle, an unassuming and partially hidden one. She had no wish to know the farmers' business, and preferred her own affairs kept private.

Och, it made her head ache. "We'll figure it out, won't we, boy? Once I'm not so tired."

Clover whinnied, his breath frosty in the cool air.

The slow clop-clopping and gentle sway of Clover's movement lulled Katy. Truly, if she didn't need to use her leg muscles to stay mounted, she would lean forward, wrap her arms around Clover, and fall asleep right there on his warm back. Safe from the chilly February wind, the insecurities of the future, and the turmoil of the present.

All she craved was to be left alone and take care of the animals.

Right. Was that truly all she desired?

The thought struck as she found Clover had returned them to the yard and Joey waited for her, leaning against his car. He looked so handsome and relaxed. Could she trust him for the safety she craved? She hadn't seen him since the night before the strike, when she'd told him her past. The farmers had been blocking the path to the Booths' processing plant every day since, and she'd heard Joey had been there making sure it stayed peaceful. So far, it had.

Today was day five. Would it be over as discussed? Is that why Joey was free to visit her? He didn't appear to be the bearer of ill news, but she hadn't heard the farmers talk about things improving or that any changes were being made. All she knew is that she would feel sick if she had to witness them dumping milk onto the side of the road. Milk that could feed hungry children. But these farmers' own children would go hungry if they didn't get the prices to change. It was too much of a muddle.

"How is Clover?" Joey met her in the yard.

"Much better." Katy found a smile as she pulled on the reins.

"May I assist you down?" Joey pressed a hand to Clover's shoulder as he looked up at her.

She nodded, a curious flutter keeping her voice silent. Joey easily lifted her to the ground, and she quickly stepped away. Too many odd sensations threatened to overwhelm her. On one hand being so near a man caused unease to skitter up her spine, especially with the recent reminder of why she fled Ireland, yet that very fear drew her toward the safety of Joey's arms.

"I came with news." Joey rubbed Clover's nose while watching her. "The strike is over."

"Oh?" Hollyhocks, what an unintelligent answer. She needed to bury the push-pull of her thoughts. They left her too dizzy and confused so that she could do little more than stare at him.

"I suspect the true reason is because farmers needed to get back to their cows, but the property damage in other counties left a strong statement." The man seemed oblivious to how his tenderness snarled her thoughts and emotions.

She forced a swallow past her dry throat. "They didn't harm Mr. Booth's property?"

Joey shook his head and, taking Clover's reins, led the way to the barn. "We took turns guarding the property overnight as well as during the day. It must have provided enough of a deterrent."

"You must be exhausted." She studied him as he opened the door with a tired chuckle. The man did look worn out. Dark circles under his green eyes. Cheeks lined and weathered. Scruff growing unevenly along his jaw. He still looked as handsome as when he cleaned up for church on Sundays. "Do you think they'll be able to find a solution?"

"I sure hope so, but if it doesn't come soon enough, people like my dad will call for another strike."

Silence fell around them as Katy removed Clover's bit and Joey picked up the curry brush. They groomed the horse together in silence. The palpable weight of Joey's fatigue hinted that he needed a horse to care for in this moment as much as she did. Clover's ears and tail relaxed for the first time since Katy brought him home. Maybe he needed the extra attention too.

Twenty minutes later, with Clover fed, watered, and content in his stall, along with food and water set for Glenn and Nessa, Joey followed Katy toward the back door of the barn. "So how have you been doing? Have you heard anything from your uncle?"

"In a way, I have." She called for Glenn and Nessa, which allowed her to avoid looking at Joey. She hadn't had a chance to tell him about Mr. Cormac, and she feared his reaction to the news as much as she craved his protection.

"So your uncle contacted you?" Hurt pierced his words. "Why didn't you tell me?"

"The strike. I didn't want to bother you." She waved Nessa to her stall. Katy predicted two weeks more until her calf came. Later than the last three years. She preferred to breed Nessa so that her calf was the first one born within the community each year. That way, she could use Nessa's milk for other needy calves if necessary. But God's creation had its own timing.

"Katy." Joey secured Glenn in his stall. "You're not a bother."

"I had cows that needed me." She gave Nessa a goodnight pat. Usually, she would return just before bed to assure herself all was good in the barn, but tonight, she needed to sleep.

"Your uncle, though."

"It wasn't my uncle." Katy's gaze lingered on the table hugging the opposite wall as she gave the barn the last look of the day. "It was a solicitor."

"And?"

"And now I know what my uncle really wants." She finished closing up the barn as she related everything Fergus Cormac told her, ending the tale at her back steps.

Joey rubbed his neck. "That's sticky. Do you know how you want to handle it?"

"I'm not faking my death."

Joey cringed. "I'm glad for that."

"And I'm not entering a loveless marriage of convenience."

"He was a cad for even suggesting such a thing."

Katy hugged herself, and not because of the cold air that slipped down her collar. "It made sense on paper, I suppose."

"Don't sell yourself short, Katy." His green eyes sparked in the waning light. "Spending the rest of your life with someone shouldn't be reduced to a business arrangement."

Katy cocked her head. "That sounds oddly personal."

He closed his eyes and sighed, his breath a cloud of white.

"You have me curious now." And a bit nervous. Was he considering such a marriage?

"It's my baby sister." Joey shoved his bare hands into his coat pockets.

Katy caught herself before relief relaxed her shoulders. *Relief?* Had she become so attached to Joey that she loathed the idea of him calling on another woman? But the idea of getting married—getting physically *close* to a man—left an ice chunk in her chest. Men only took from her. How could she consider something more with him?

"I learned this morning that she would welcome Andy Booth calling on her. I feel like a go-between, carrying letters between Romeo and Juliet. That didn't work out well in the script, and I have my doubts about this arrangement too. Both fathers are going to be angry when they learn of it. Sometimes I wish I could shake some common sense into people."

"Sometimes we have to learn it on our own," she whispered.

Joey narrowed his gaze. "And you didn't answer my question. Have you decided what you want to do?"

Katy paced toward her garden. Ran away, more like. The garlic shoots waved in the wind. The rest was hardened clumps of dirt. She needed to focus on the real problem, not on the crack developing in her emotional armor. "I reckon it's not a plan, but I want Mr. Cormac to tell my uncle he can have the land if he'll leave me alone."

"You think that will work?"

"If it doesn't, I'll offer the money too."

Joey stopped her with a hand on her arm. The concern that had been her undoing the other day showed on his face. His presence spoke of safety, protection. Could she trust him to be unlike every other man—besides their grandfathers—and have her best interests at heart?

"I feel guilty for willingly handing over Daideó's money without a fight." She latched onto his gorgeous green eyes, drawing strength to spill the thought that haunted her. "He saved it for me, but now it's the price of me freedom. I mayn't be witherin' away in a laundry like me *máthair*, but maybe I be in a prison all me own."

CHAPTER 8

Joey blinked against the onslaught of words. He struggled to keep up, and the faster Katy talked, the stronger her accent became. He leaned in, trying to follow, unable to split his attention between her and their darkening surroundings.

The emotion pouring out of her tugged him in like a spiraling eddy. Her words took on a lyrical tang so that they hardly sounded like English. He watched her mouth, trying to interpret the words she used, but that distracted him entirely.

Honestly, he wasn't sure how he'd found himself so close to her, and that awareness stopped him inches away from kissing her. That's when he realized she'd fallen silent, her blue eyes searching for … something. Even if he knew what it was, he wasn't sure if he could give it to her. She must need comfort, right? Emotional turmoil laced her tone. But that wasn't what he was picking up on.

Disquiet? Yes. Timidity? Yes. Fear?

He froze. Like a swift undercurrent, that emotion churned beneath all others.

Never would he wish to scare her. No matter how hard he found it to be, he would put space between them.

"Joey?" Her voice was a whisper, her breath brushing his chin. Curious, questioning. It wrapped around him and tugged him to close the distance.

As he touched her lips, she squealed, and a solid slap landed on his cheek. He jumped back, as if bitten by a snake, scrambling to get his mind working on all cylinders.

What had he done?

"I'm so sorry." Katy's voice shook, tears welled in her eyes, and her hands hovered between covering her mouth and cheeks. "I—"

"Don't." Joey shook his head. He pushed away the chaotic tangle of electricity racing through him to focus on her.

"But—"

Joey held up a hand. "Don't apologize." Tears slipped down her cheeks, and Joey felt them like punches to the stomach. He eased closer, and when she didn't flinch, he reached for her. "I'm the one who's sorry."

She shook her head but sobbed harder. Unsure what else to do, he pulled her to his chest and wrapped her in his arms. He rested his chin on her head, the coarse strands of her hair catching on his stubble. His heart broke for her, for what he did to her. How could he have forgotten himself and caused so much pain? And why did she let him comfort her?

Finally, she pulled away, drying her cheeks with the edge of her sleeve.

"Katy?" He needed to know. "Can you tell me? Was it me or the kiss you didn't want?"

She gave him a tiny, watery smile. "It wasn't you."

Okay. Good. "And the kiss?"

Her face crumpled.

Horsefeathers. "Katy, I'm—"

She waved him to a stop. "It wasn't your kiss." She sniffed as if trying to stay composed. She needn't for him. "It was me. It was my memories."

Father God, no. The fear he'd seen in her eyes. This explained it. His imagination raced down paths that left him nauseated and furious.

"No one has ever wanted to kiss me without expecting a whole lot more." Katy spoke slowly, her accent under full control. "It's the same reason my mother was sent to the Magdalene Laundry. We're too pretty.

We tempt men. She had me without a husband, so I've known any … interactions are all my fault."

"Stop." Joey spoke more sharply than he intended and forced his tone to soften. "They're not your fault."

"Regardless, I discovered a well-placed slap saved me more times than I can count."

His heart skipped a beat. "No one took advantage?"

"They tried, but the slap usually gave me enough time to put distance between us."

Joey let out a somewhat easier breath. He wished he could corral each of those men and show them what an unwanted touch felt like. With a whip, preferably.

"You're the first man I …"

The sweetness in those words washed away his tension, and he smiled. Tentatively, he reached to cup her cheek. "Thank you, Katy."

She startled, staring up at him with round eyes. "For what?"

"For trusting me."

"I do, Joey. It's all so new … confusing." She leaned into his touch. "Now what?"

He tugged her into a hug again. She came willingly, much to his heart's comfort. He hadn't caused too much damage if she allowed him to hold her, right? He adjusted his arms so they fully wrapped around her, enveloping her. She leaned her head against his chest and his protective instinct to surge like an ungrounded electrical current.

Heaven help him, he cared for this woman. More than he reckoned.

He looked into the dusky sky, his thoughts a vow. He would protect her. No one would take advantage of her again.

Including himself. As much as he yearned to keep her within the circle of his arms, the embrace needed to end. He tilted his chin to look down at her, stalling. The trust that flashed in her eyes galvanized him.

He cracked a grin. "Now I teach you what to do if a slap doesn't work."

"What?" Katy couldn't stop the laughter that trailed onto her word. His suggestion seemed to come out of nowhere, especially with the intensity radiating from him.

"'Round these parts, there are a lot more open spaces, which makes it harder to hide or escape. I don't want you unable to defend yourself, especially with the threat of your uncle hanging over us."

Us. Nestled deeper in Joey's arms, Katy sure liked the sound of that. She liked the feel of this hug too. Frankly, if she gave herself a moment to be honest, the kiss might keep her up tonight. Never had she experienced something so sweet. Then she had to ruin it.

"Let's teach you a few things." Joey took her hand and laid it to his stubbled cheek. The cheek she'd slapped.

"It's red!" How could she have hit him? Not Joey. She felt safe with Joey. It had been purely reactionary. A reflex. Her stomach clenched and she dropped her chin.

"I'll be just fine." He gave her a smile that slowed her thoughts and patted the hand he held to his cheek. "As you said, slaps will usually stun someone, but also make them angry so that they grab your wrist. Like this." Joey moved his hand down her arm until his fingers wrapped around her wrist, making her arm seem frail, thin.

Katy swallowed.

"His focus will be on the point of contact—your right arm. That means, you need to use your left foot."

"To do what?" Her heart pounded in her head, throwing off her concentration.

"Stomp. Hard." He winked. "See how when I grab your wrist, I aim to pull you toward me? Instead of letting that get you off balance, use the momentum to stomp harder. Try it."

"I can't hurt you."

"I've been stomped on by a cow. You won't hurt me."

"That's not comforting."

Joey laughed. "Come on, try it. On three, I'll pull you toward me."

Katy nodded. On three, he tugged, and she landed her heel on his instep.

Joey hissed. "You've got a heel on that boot."

"I'm sorry!" She jumped back.

"No. That's good." He kept a gentle hold on her arm. "You want to cause pain."

"Not to you."

"I'll feel better if I know you can handle yourself. Lil and Amy grew up with brothers, and Lily can shoot a shotgun better than me. I know they can handle themselves. Your turn to learn."

"I'm not one of your sisters."

"No, you most definitely are not. So don't hold back. Please." He cleared his throat of the emotion lacing his words. "After you stomp, you'll have bent them over, giving you aim to land an elbow in their nose."

"I'm not going to—"

"If it's your life on the line, you will. That's my point, Katy. Someone determined to harm you needs to be dealt with and not compassionately. Understand?"

Again she nodded.

"Good. Now, from the slap." He replaced her right hand on his cheek. "Ready?"

She patted his cheek. Och, she couldn't do it. Not to him.

"Katy!"

"I cannot hit you again."

"Yes, you can. I need to know you'll be safe."

"How can I not be safe when I have you protecting me?"

"You're insufferable." He grinned. "And fortunate you're so adorable."

Cold squeezed Katy's heart. "W-what did you say?"

Joey froze, uncertainty cutting through his humor. "What did I say?"

Her breaths came in shallow gasps. She could trust Joey. She couldn't let his words shake her like this. "Y-you cannot tell me I'm pretty."

He blinked.

He didn't understand. She backed away from him. How could he not see? Why had she thought this might work? Why had she let her herself hope, even for a moment? She knew better than to trust a man.

His eyes widened. "Oh, Katy, I'm so sorry! I'm a blockhead. I didn't mean it the way it sounded. Now that I hear the words I used, I realize it's the worst thing I could have said. I didn't mean that if you weren't adorable, I would feel differently. I was teasing you."

"Maybe I don't want to be teased." Another step back, with her heart trying to pound out of her chest. "Maybe being *adorable* isn't funny."

"Katy, I'm sorry."

"D-did you only kiss me because I'm pretty?"

His mouth flopped open.

She began to tremble. This was what happened to her mother. How it started. Why the townspeople had warned their men about her. "D-did you only teach me to defend myself because you wanted to hold my hand?"

His face paled.

Black edged her vision as anger rose over her panic. "There's a reason I haven't married. I'm not like Lily who loves her independence. I'm not married because of men like you."

"Katy, please. I care about you because you're smart and sweet and shy. Pretty, too—I can't lie about that—but it wasn't the reason I kissed you. And yes, I could hold you all night. Not because I would treat you selfishly, but because you deserve to feel safe and I—"

She couldn't listen to any more. She couldn't sort through the truth and what she feared he said only because he thought she wanted to hear it. "Because you're a police officer, I'd still appreciate being able to tell you if Mr. Cormac or my uncle contacts me again. Otherwise, let's you and me go back to you simply being my friend's brother."

She squeezed her fingers into tight fists. The words hurt to say. Losing his connection felt like the slice of an incision. But she needed to think—needed to know he wasn't like every other man who only craved one thing—and she couldn't do that with him so close to her. He made her feel things that scared her. What if he wasn't as good as he sounded?

"If you wish." Joey nodded, his jaw tight. "Just promise me one thing."

A promise? What did he want from her?

"If you need anything, you will come see me. Please."

She stared at him, wishing to believe everything he said, but how could she? Other than Daideó and Lily's grandfather, no other man had ever looked out for her well-being with no ulterior motivation.

Doubt and fear swirled together, rooting her feet to the ground. Joey closed the distance between them, sadness wrapping him like a cloak. Was she doing the right thing?

"I'm sorry, Katy." He gently squeezed her shoulder. "I know I broke your trust, but please, I'm here if you need me. For any reason. No strings attached. I promise."

Joey's sincerity seeped into her heart. Had she just pushed one of the few good men away for good? Even if he did think she was pretty. Night closed around her, but she didn't let her tears loose until Joey's headlights faded from sight.

CHAPTER 9

Friday, May 12, 1933, 11 weeks later

Katy wiped her sleeve across her forehead. The noonday sun beat down on her freshly seeded garden—a garden that was supposed to grow her medicinal herbs and provide her food for the winter. It would if the seeds actually took in the dry ground. This was the seventh trip with two pails of water she'd carried over from the pump, and she'd only managed to water four and a half rows.

The unusually warm week gave the false promise of summer. By the time the seeds sprouted, the threat of one last frost should have dissipated—though she'd seen snow fall in mid-May several times—but the dry spring did not bode well for a robust harvest.

Her small hay field looked even scragglier than it had the past few lean years. Dust swirled in the air whenever a gust of wind blew across the freshly plowed fields. An even weaker crop than normal could negate her effort to expand the plot. Then how would she feed Clover, Glenn, Nessa, and Nessa's calf? As it was, most of her income from the spring calving season went toward Clover's upkeep alone.

She'd even taken in her own dresses at the side seams so no one would notice—especially Lily who might report to Joey—the weight she'd lost while reducing her meals to twice a day in order to save money. At least until she heard from Mr. Cormac, who hadn't made another appearance, leading her to wonder if perhaps the whole story had been a hoax.

Katy trudged back to the pump, grateful she'd decided to wear one of her flour sack dresses instead of her veterinarian ensemble of split-skirt and fitted jacket. The idea of the heavy, dark cotton fabric made sweat break out on her back. She downed a double handful of water before working the pump handle to refill the buckets. Grasping each pail handle, she waddled back to the garden and carefully distributed the water over the mound covering the carrot seeds.

She was just finishing watering the fifth row when a car pulled into her yard. She ran her sleeve over her face, the grit scratching her skin. She should have splashed her face when she'd taken a drink. Lily and Joey's dad unfolded his lanky form as he exited his truck. Katy hurried to meet him.

"Good day, Mr. Moore. Can I help you?"

"I hope so." He swiped the hat from his head. "Some of my cows are having udder trouble. I was able to help a few, but the three most recently calved need more help than I can give them."

"I'd be happy to come have a look. I'll gather my things and drive over." She smiled despite her apprehension. Joey often visited his parents' farm—would she see him today? Would she like to?

Over the past months, he'd kept his distance like he promised, but she found she missed him. He'd drive past her place in his police car every couple days, never stopping, and on her more lonely days, she wished he would. Why hadn't she been able to trust him when she had a chance? If only she could make the fear go away.

"My sons and I are working our south field, so just go on in the barn when you get there. I'll settle up with you later." He glanced toward the barn. "How's your supply of feed for that horse?"

"Still using the several bales another farmer gave me for taking care of his sow."

"Broader, if I'm not mistaken."

Katy smiled. She wouldn't say, but he was correct. Mrs. Broader sent her home with a pot pie, too, even though Katy could tell the family couldn't spare either the hay or the food.

"Has Wallace been to see you?"

Clover's previous owner? "He has not. Should I be watching for him?"

Mr. Moore rubbed his neck, looking so much like his son. "He's been kicking up more nonsense than usual. Nothing specific, mind you, just enough to cast doubt on how you acquired the horse."

"Which I bought and have the paperwork to prove."

Mr. Moore held up his hands. "I know, but he's changing his tune now that his bank loan for that John Deere is higher than he thought. His tendency is to play an angle for easy money, so he may try something underhanded to get his now-healthy horse back for free in order to sell the tractor."

And in Katy's experience, people rarely sided with the female when up against even a dubious male. A distinct wishing for Joey to be on her side rose within her. Could she count on help from him after pushing him away? If not, she'd finally gotten a chance to contact a lawyer about her grandfather's inheritance—not that she'd heard anything from him in weeks. She doubted help would come from that quarter, whether against her uncle or whatever nefarious plan Mr. Wallace was hatching.

"I'll keep my ears open, but his actions will be in direct relation to how desperate he feels." Mr. Moore replaced his hat, cutting off her train of thought. "After you see to my cows, there are a couple other farms worth visiting. They think they can handle it on their own, but their cows are having the same symptoms as mine."

Katy frowned. "Udder infections aren't likely to spread through a community. They are rarely contagious and usually occur due to poor conditions, which is rare on farms with experienced dairymen like yourself." *Unless the strike business distracted them.*

"Flattery isn't necessary, Dr. Wells." Mr. Moore waved away her words, tugging his hat onto his head. "I know full well what causes them and how deadly they can be if left uncorrected. We'll talk more this afternoon when I get in from the fields."

Katy left her garden to change out of her cooler dress, mulling over what was likely a difficult case of mastitis, but the possibility of seeing

Joey pushed to the forefront of her thoughts. Each time she'd encountered him over the past three months, at church or in town, all she could remember was how much she hoped he'd kiss her again. And it was exactly that thinking that would land her in a Magdalene Laundry, just like her mother.

The Moore's yard was deserted when Katy parked her truck near the barn. If Mrs. Moore was about, she didn't make her presence known. Katy cast a wistful glance toward her friend's property, across the couple fields of corn seedlings that stood between them. How long had it been since they had a chat in front of Lily's fireplace?

Katy desired nothing more than to talk to her friend about Joey, but as twins, those two were closest of all the Moore siblings, and Katy refused to come between them, especially since the Moore family seemed in turmoil. Andy Booth was calling on Joey and Lily's little sister, Amy, and the whole town could talk of nothing else. The added pressure on Lily to marry before Amy had Lily talking only about the new puppy she planned to get.

She supposed she could tell Lily about Mr. Cormac and Uncle Patrick's threat, but with silence on that front, what was there really to share with her distracted friend? Anyway, the Magdalene Laundry threat was one she never told anyone.

Anyone except Joey.

Katy pushed into the barn, frustrated at how her past held her captive. Too pretty, everyone had told her. Dark black hair that matched no one in the village, which could only mean it belonged to her father, an unknown person about whom the villagers delighted to create fanciful stories, none flattering to either Katy or her mother. Nevertheless, Katy had her refuge in Daideó and his veterinary practice. She smiled, thinking of him. If he were here in the Moore's barn, he would speak to each animal by name, from the big sow in the corner, to the tabby cat that lurked in the rafters, to the ill cows singled out to stay in the main barn, away from the others of the herd.

Katy made her way toward them—three cows in all, each having delivered a calf four to six weeks ago. Peeking over the edge of each stall door, it took her only a glance to confirm they were unwell. Dull eyes and rough coats spoke to their body's struggle against infection. Red udders and awkward stances testified of their discomfort. And not a one chewed their cud.

Most farmers knew tricks to prevent or calm mastitis, but some infections got out of control and led to the death of the animal. Not to mention, an infected udder meant tainted milk. Tainted milk meant the cow was not earning her keep. If that couldn't be remedied, the cow was retired from dairy service at best. With the lack of movement on milk prices, sick cows would make the matter so much worse.

Katy led the first cow into the aisle and tethered her to a post. Then, gliding her hand along the flank, she worked her way to the udder, squatting to see better, and finding it warmer and harder than it should be. The cow stomped her discomfort.

"Easy, girl." Katy rested her forehead on the cow's belly. "I know this feels miserable. We'll get you right as rain again in no time."

"That's quite the promise." Joey's voice nearly startled Katy into losing her balance and falling onto her backside.

"Joey Moore, ya should be ashamed of yourself, scaring a girl like that." Her burr came out strong. Katy dusted her skirt as she stood, hiding her trembling behind the cow's bulk.

He frowned. "You know that wasn't my intention, right?"

"Hollyhocks. What do ya need?" She planted her hands on her hips, a mite too defensive and vulnerable here in his father's barn to hear much of anything from him.

"Came for my daily jug of milk and saw your truck." He patted the cow's shoulder as he approached. "Something wrong with the cows?"

"Infection in the udder." Katy squatted again, reaching under the cow to give milking a try. The cow stomped and mooed, obviously in distress.

"The milk stream is light for one of Dad's cows." Joey squatted beside her. "Before Dad got the electric milker, we'd milk the herd by hand, and I'd fill a pail in no time flat. He has an eye for a good milk cow."

"And he knows how to treat the usual udder maladies. This is an acute case of mastitis, and he said something about other cows on other farms showing similar problems."

"That's odd. It's not contagious or something, right?"

"No, not like a cold would be." Katy turned as she spoke and found Joey much closer than she expected. His green eyes widened as if he hadn't expected her so close either. Yet neither moved.

Katy's heart thrummed in her ears. The cow stomped. Her tail swatted Katy's head, leaving a piece of scratchy straw on her cheek.

Joey dashed it away with his thumb, fast enough she barely felt it, before cupping her elbow and helping her to her feet.

Katy cleared her throat. "There are two more cows I need to see to before I settle on a treatment."

Joey just blinked at her. What was he thinking behind that pensive expression?

"Joey?" She pressed into the cow's side.

"Can we talk again?"

Katy's lips parted, but she had no words to say. The question tumbled inside her head and her heart, leaving her bewildered.

"About this." Joey wagged a finger between them.

Right. She knew that. Her ready defenses warned her to say *no*, but her every fiber begged to say *yes*.

"Katy?"

"I don't know."

The whispered words felt like a knife, splitting her in two. She desperately wanted to explore these feelings, yet her skin prickled with unease. Her history stood between them like a boulder and fear that any choice would be the wrong one had her turning away from him.

Why wasn't the whole matter more clear after three months away from this man? Was it possible to feel more strongly attached to him after their separation? It made no sense to her and she needed it laid out like a scientific equation. One the one hand, her heart said to trust him, depend on him, whereas on the other, her head clamored that she was just like her mother, a woman who only deserved to be sent to a Magdalene Laundry.

So, what was she supposed to do?

CHAPTER 10

Joey stepped back, giving Katy the space she seemed to need. He hadn't gone a day without thinking about her these past weeks. Each time he let himself drive by her house, however, he chose not to knock on her door. Chose to honor her wish to be left alone. He assured himself she was safe, but from afar.

Until today, of course. He hadn't meant to get so close. Wasn't even sure how it happened. But it had, and now he was sure there was something between them. He had to ask. Had to try again. But the mere question, just asking if they could talk, seemed to tie Katy in knots.

If only he knew how to help.

Countless times these last weeks, he'd nearly spilled everything to Lil. Could she give him understanding? Or at least help him to know what to do? But Lily wasn't just his twin—she was Katy's dearest friend. He wouldn't take that away from Katy by skewing Lil toward his side of the dilemma. No, he was on his own to figure this out.

And it was time to act.

"Katy?" He stretched a tentative hand toward her shoulder, hoping to gauge her reaction to his touch. "What can I do?"

She shook her head. "It's not about you or even something you can fix."

His hand landed and she didn't flinch. "Then can you at least talk to me?"

She studied him for a full minute, measuring him. He held his breath, the weight of the moment bore down on him like a charging bull. Whatever she chose, he would honor her choice, no matter how much it hurt. If she pushed him away, it simply meant she wasn't ready, and maybe she never would be. Her reserve, her wounds, did not reflect on him as a person.

She covered the hand he rested on her shoulder with her own and nodded.

Relief coursed through him.

A faint smile lifted her lips. "Why aren't you a dairy farmer, Joey Moore? You look … good here." She ducked her head, but it failed to hide her blush.

How he wanted to respond to her sweet flirt, but he absorbed the question like a punch to the stomach, stepped backward, and nearly tripped over his own heels. The cow mooed at his abrupt behavior, and the pig snorted from the pen behind him.

Confusion twisted Katy's face. "I shouldn't have asked?"

"It's all right." He tried to set her at ease as a strange panic welled in his chest. With the next breath, he spit out his usual answer. "I'm a policeman and can't do both jobs."

"I'm so sorry. I didn't—'twas just a question."

It was more than a question. It was her offering an olive branch and he mucked it up by not effectively protecting his vulnerable underbelly. The irony of his desire for her to open up to him stiffened his spine and he folded his arms against the sharp pain in his chest. "So it was."

"Joey Moore, what do you take me for?" Her eyes sparked. "Spilling my secrets without getting any in return? Hollyhocks. I won't stand for that. If you'd like to explore *this*,"—she mimicked him pointing between them—"then don't treat me as if I can't handle your secrets too. Obviously, there is more to you not being a dairy farmer than being unable to *do both jobs*."

Heaven help him, she'd hit the proverbial nail dead on. The cow beside them stared at him as if daring him to be a man—to stand before Katy with a bared heart or be a coward and walk away. Did he desire to see where *this* went? Yes, yes he absolutely did. Would being fully honest with Katy make her run worse than before? *You won't know until you try.*

He rubbed the back of his neck. Was he as brave as she?

Katy left Joey to make his decision as she squatted beside the cow and rubbed infection-fighting ointment onto the cow's udder. She respected Joey's turmoil, but wouldn't give him an easy way out. Not if he desired to build trust between them.

Honestly, the question hadn't been meant as a gauntlet. She'd actually been attempting a compliment. His broad shoulders framed by the weathered barn walls cast a wonderfully protective image that caused warmth to fill her like Daideó's coffee. However, Joey's reaction had flagged the question as important. Now she needed to know what he hid, or how could she trust him with more of her secrets?

She frowned as she completed her ministrations. There was talk of a new treatment for mastitis—a treatment for any infection, really, human or animal—called an antibiotic. About six years ago, a professor by the name of Alexander Fleming had discovered something called penicillin, but Katy wouldn't feel right passing along the cost of the medicine until she knew for certain it would work. If she had that inheritance, this was another way she could use the money.

"It's not that I don't admire dairy farmers." Joey handed her an empty pail and slipped a milking stool beneath her, helping her sit with a gentle touch.

Was he finally about to open up to her? She gave him an encouraging smile and his hand lingered on her arm before he stepped back. She turned her attention to milking, hiding her flushed face against the cow's side.

"Farming is hard work." Joey spoke slowly, quietly. "It takes its toll. Especially now."

She waited for him to continue, but when he didn't, she attempted a prompt. "I reckon hard work isn't why you chose not to be a farmer."

"True."

Katy passed him the full pail, unease growing at Joey's reticence. She instructed him to dump the bad milk while she put the cow in her stall and brought out the next one.

Joey returned, swinging the empty pail. "I miss it sometimes."

She ducked under the second cow to rub in the ointment. His statement sparked an idea. What if she gave him a task? Perhaps he would talk to her then. She sat free of the cow, resting her elbows on her knees. "Milk this one, won't you?"

Joey raised his eyebrows, but Katy pushed to her feet and secured the third cow farther down the aisle, then massaged ointment in the cow's udder while she waited for Joey to get his hands busy to see if her hypothesis was correct.

"I want to do good for people. Help people." The splash of milk in the pail and the cow's moos of discomfort punctuated Joey's words. "I used to have to stand up for Lily when we were in school. The other boys teased her, and I hated it. One day, it came to blows. Bloody nose, dirt-stained, scraped up, the whole bit. Lily found me sitting in the barn waiting for my punishment from Dad for getting into a fight. Without a word, she handed me the peppermint stick she'd been hoarding since Christmas."

"She does love her peppermint."

"Of course, I refused it, but she said something that day that stuck with me. She said I was like a moat. Nice-looking, even peaceful, unless someone tried to attack what I guarded." He chuckled. "It's not that I can't help people as a farmer. It's just how my dad chooses to farm makes it so much like a business that it's lost its personal quality."

"Farming is your father's business, Joey."

She came to take the pail from him, but he held onto the handle, looking up at her. "I know, but do we really need electricity? Plumbing? A tractor? Do we need to keep expanding?"

"Go on and dump this." Katy pushed him toward the barn door, the irony of dumping milk not lost on her. She quickly put the second cow in her stall, then moved the third cow up the aisle. When he returned, she busied herself collecting her medical supplies so Joey would take the hint and start milking. He did. And she prompted him to start talking again. "You aren't a fan of progress?"

"It's not that." Joey huffed.

She knew that tone. The hemming and hawing over telling her why he didn't want to be like his dad all made sense now. "Joey, you can tell me the story."

His eyes popped wide. "What story?"

"About the day you decided you weren't going to be a farmer like your father."

He stared at her as if she'd turned into a cow.

"Come, now. There's a story there. Out with it." She rested her medical bag on the top corner of an empty stall.

"Katy, I can't do this." He jumped to his feet. The cow stomped, kicking the milk pail over. "I know you hope I'll open up, but I can't."

"It's just little ol' me." She laid both her hands on his shoulders, like he was wont to do to her. She let herself sink into the green depths of his eyes for only a moment. "What makes you the protector that you are, Joey Moore? Tell me that story as you milk this poor cow. Milk and talk."

Joey gave just the hint of a smile before returning to his milking stool and resting his forehead against the cow's belly. "I was fourteen. It was spring after a particularly long, cold winter. Mud everywhere. Shoes too tight. Pants too short. Mom took us to town to get supplies. She never talked about money, but as my sisters admired the fabric in the store, I saw my mom counting coins and a tear slipping down her cheek."

Katy adjusted herself out of his peripheral vision so she could watch him without him realizing it. A muscle along his jaw moved, betraying the emotion behind this story. This was his heart, and Katy held her arms close to her own as if she held his there too.

"Mom managed to maneuver Lil and Amy away from the fabric, but

I put it together that she didn't have enough to buy the cloth. When I went to give her my pennies, Dad walked in and I overheard him talking to the store owner—I forget his name, but he's since moved on—about the new tractor John Deere had come out with, The Waterloo Boy."

She could picture the mechanical beast with the monstrous wheels and loud engine.

"That night, Mom caught her dress on a snag and ripped a right fine hole in the fabric—the kind that she always warned me was hard to patch. I had plenty of them on my clothes. I knew she needed—no, deserved—a new dress, but all Dad could talk about was that awful tractor." Joey's voice caught.

Katy stayed perfectly still.

"That night, I heard them fighting. It was the only fight I ever heard them have. To this day, I can't say they ever fought again, but that night, it was the loudest, angriest fight. Dad won, I suppose, because Mom patched her dress, and Dad got a tractor. That day, I also decided I would never let something new come in the way of taking care of my mother and sisters."

Katy's heart ached. "You be a good man, Joey Moore."

He glanced at her. "You've said that before."

"Right. I have. Because I believe it." She blinked away the evidence of emotion clouding her eyes. Truly, how had she ever doubted this man? Why had she pushed him away? "I haven't known many of the good ones."

He set the pail aside and stood before her, abashed and discomfited. "You deserve someone good, Katy. Better than just good. I—"

"Och. Don't go putting words in me mouth. I know exactly the type of good man I admire." Why hadn't she seen it before? "A good man is someone willing to stand up for someone else."

He rubbed his neck as he searched her eyes.

Katy looked away. "I'm sorry for not trusting you."

He turned her chin so she had to meet his gaze. "No one had proved that you could trust them—least of all a man like me, so who was I to ask that of you? And I won't ask it of you now. I want to prove to you that I'm trustworthy first."

"Right." Katy placed her hand on the cheek she'd smacked nearly three months ago. "I have no doubt that you will."

CHAPTER 11

Joey's heart flipped in his chest at the admiration shining in Katy's eyes. He hadn't told anyone, even Lil, that he'd overhead that fight between their parents, but it shaped every decision he made after that. Katy was right about him—he would put himself between the defenseless and … anyone. Did that make him a good man?

Words tangled in his throat—a welcome thing since his dad's voice called out in the yard. He grabbed the half-empty milk pail and met the man outside the barn, leaving Katy and part of his heart inside.

"What's that?" His father raised a brow at the pail.

"Bad milk." Joey tossed it across the dirt beside the barn wall. "Katy has me milking while she does whatever miracle work she does."

Both brows rose. "She put you to work, eh?"

"Now she can put you to work." Joey shoved the pail into his father's hands.

Dad turned away without it. "You have a system. Don't let me interrupt. In fact, you finish up while I speak with her."

Joey held in a sigh behind his dad's back but followed him into the barn. Katy had put the cow he'd milked into her stall and was leaning over a stall railing, talking to the pig. Never had she looked more appealing and fun and—

"Dr. Wells." Dad blocked Joey's view. "What's the verdict?"

Joey waffled. There was no reason to stay in the barn, but he hesitated to go wash out the pail instead of listening to be sure his dad treated

Katy the way she deserved. He shook his head. Telling that story had him on high alert for any injustice.

"The cow in the farthest stall should be fine in no time, Mr. Moore. Her infection appears limited to one quarter." Katy straightened and gathered her medical bag. "The others have three or four udder quarters infected. They need to be milked as frequently as possible and the milk thrown out. The ointment will help, but if their condition doesn't improve in a day or so, I'd like to try something stronger. It's a new—"

"Will they be better by Monday?" Dad planted his hands on his hips, and Joey had to work to keep his mouth shut.

"I can't really say." She walked two steps toward the door. "Why?"

Dad glanced over at Joey. "I suppose you'll hear it soon enough. We're voting tonight on whether to join the strike in the morning."

So many questions sputtered in Joey's head, but Katy managed to ask hers first, and with much more calm than Joey ever would have managed. "Who will take care of your cows?"

"Don't you worry about that." Dad led them out into the bright May sunshine. "If we don't get the milk and butter prices raised, more farms will go out of business. Good farmers will be left without income and homes for their families. I won't let that happen on my watch. We have to band together. Demand fair prices. It's worked for other unions across the nation, and it'll work for us too."

"It didn't in February." Joey failed to calm his mounting frustration. Frustration at his dad, at the Booths, at the government, at the injustice. "All it got you was a bunch of empty promises."

"Which is why we're doing it again."

"You two can debate the merits of a strike later." Katy gripped her medical bag with both hands. "I'll return tomorrow to check on my patients, but you need to milk them every couple hours. Is that clear, Mr. Moore? If you let this infection spread, it—"

"I know what it can do!" Dad silenced her. "As if we need one more thing to threaten our livelihood."

"That's not Katy's fault." Joey put himself between them. "You didn't have to stretch yourself so thin you can't manage now. That's on you."

"It put food in your belly, young man." Dad shoved a finger into Joey's chest.

"Horsefeathers and applesauce!" Lily materialized beside them, green eyes sparking, her curly, black-haired dog beside her. "I could hear both of you shouting halfway through the cornfield. What is going on?"

"They're striking again." Joey knocked his dad's hand away. Meeting his twin's gaze, he let their silent communication fill in the information. Her brown braid slipped over her shoulder as she reached down to scratch behind her dog's floppy ear.

"So Amy and Andy…" Lily glanced at Katy, who gave her friend a smile.

"Good, you're here." Mom joined their circle, apron dusted with flour. "At the moment, Amy and Andy are just fine. However, Lily, if you would have considered Andy Booth as a husband, it would make all of this so much simpler."

"Mother!" Joey couldn't believe what he was hearing. He might not like his twin living on her own, but he wouldn't let her get railroaded by their mother and her matchmaking.

"Don't chide me, Joseph Moore, you—" Mom cut him short as she stared at Lily. "What are you wearing, young lady?"

Lily looked down at her usual jeans and flannel, the red of which matched her cheeks. "You said to come to dinner."

"Yes. Mr. and Mrs. Anderson are coming, and so are their older children, including Simon."

A quiet gasp escaped from Katy as Lily's expression changed so many shades in a matter of moments.

Joey rubbed the back of his neck. "Mom, you didn't."

"It's for your own good." Mom wrapped the edge of her apron in her hands. "It's time you got serious about getting married. Amy is nearly engaged."

Dad growled. "She is not."

"She is, and it's not proper for an older sister not to marry first." Mom wagged the towel at Lily. "You will go home and get dressed appropriately, then be here to welcome them for dinner. Is that clear?"

As Lily's skin washed out to a dull gray, Katy's hand on his arm stopped the words threatening to spew from his mouth. Mom glared at Lily, but Dad caught Katy's action, and Joey froze. This matchmaking conversation could not turn his direction. Not with the fragile ground between him and Katy.

"Fine. I'll wear a dress." Lily spun on her boot, headed for the cornfield, her dog trotting to keep up.

"I have more patients to see." Katy spoke quietly and gave his arm a gentle squeeze. "If you'll excuse me. Mrs. Moore, gentleman, a pleasure."

She left his side, then, and Joey floated unmoored in a sea of conflicting emotions. Who to protect and who to stand against. Where to place his loyalties. One certainty surfaced—if he wanted to protect the feelings budding between him and Katy, they had to be kept secret from his family and their interfering nonsense.

Katy hurried after Lily and her dog, not catching up to her until they were standing in the middle of a freshly seeded cornfield. "Lily, wait, please."

"It's humiliating." Unshed tears made the green in Lily's eyes sparkle like emeralds. Her dog pressed against her leg, and she rested a hand on its head.

"I'm sorry for it." Katy grasped for the right words to support her friend.

"Why must everyone think I have to get married? Let alone, before Amy does? I'm happy as I am."

"Are you?" Katy cocked her head. "Happy, I mean?"

"Of course. I have my dogs, my farm." She waved her hand in the direction of her property. "What else could I need?"

"Companionship? A friend?"

"Ah, but I have my dogs and I have you." Lily smiled. "Speaking of which, you haven't been by in a while. Is everything all right?"

"I'm fine," Katy tightened her grip on her medical bag. "But we weren't talking about me."

"Uh-huh. Time for you to talk to me, and I'm not leaving until you do, which means I'll be late to dinner. I certainly don't mind, but my mother will have your head if she learns you're the reason why."

Stubborn woman. Katy had no doubt Lily would follow through on her threat. Could she tell her about Joey?

Lily leaned closer, earnestness pouring from her. "I'm here for you. You know that, right?"

"I do." Katy blinked back the unexpected tears. "It's hard to remember who your friends are sometimes. Especially when the unexpected happens. Like a man showing up—"

"A man?" Lily's eyes widened. "From where? Who?"

Katy laughed despite the sob that caught in her throat. "You'll let me tell the story, won't you?"

Lily waved her on.

"Right. His name is Fergus Cormac. He's from Ireland."

Lily frowned. "You don't talk much about your past. You knew him then?"

"I don't remember him, but he remembers me. Tracked me down, actually. I don't … I don't trust him." And that was the honest truth, a truth burdening her more than the fact she wasn't in a hurry to tell Lily she was beginning to care for her brother.

"Next time he comes around, have Joey send him on his way."

Katy startled, but Lily kept talking as if she hadn't noticed.

"You know he'd do anything to keep us women safe." Lily flashed a tolerating smile. "He can be annoying that way."

"It's sweet how he looks out for you."

Lily scrunched her nose. "I've had about enough of it lately."

"And if circumstances were different and this Irishman was actually someone I liked …" Katy held her breath, hiding her real question in this one.

"I'd be happy for you, Katy. But only if you were truly happy. I only desire the best person for you, and if you don't trust this man, then I'm against him on principle." She sighed. "You know I'm not against women getting married. I just don't want to. I'm perfectly happy as I am. You've never wanted to marry, either, as I recall. If you found someone you trust, would you rethink your stance?"

"No." The answer came too hastily, almost as a reflex. She chuckled to hide her discomfort. "I don't dwell on the past, and the future is mine alone to do as I wish. It's why I came to America, after all, and you, my dearest friend, have helped me remember."

Lily studied her for a moment longer. "If you say so."

"I do. Now I have rounds early in the morning, especially if they decide to strike, and you have a dinner to get to."

"Don't remind me." Lily rolled her eyes, then grew serious. "Is there anything I can do to help?"

Katy shook her head. "I might come calling for some of your hot chocolate, though."

"I would be angry with you if you didn't." Lily pulled her into a hug. "We'll make it through this, Katy. Both of us."

Katy squeezed, infusing every ounce of hope into the embrace she could.

That night, Joey slipped into the assembly hall. Pandemonium reigned. Farmers shouting at other farmers. The mayor's gavel beating a steady rhythm. Fortunately, a different officer had been called to keep the peace, but the poor man was in over his head.

Putting his fingers against his lips, Joey let loose the shrill whistle that silenced the room as effectively as the last time. He gave a silent nod to the mayor, then leaned against the back wall, arms and ankles crossed, determined to stay out of the way. A more conversant—albeit spirited—dialogue commenced, and Joey struggled with what the farmers said.

He hated the idea of agreeing with his father, but from what he could gather, only a demonstration would give voice to the farmers. Yet Joey had seen it before—these strikes never stayed peaceful. Was violence the only answer?

The door beside him opened, and a dark figure slipped inside. Joey straightened, drawing the figure's attention.

"Ah, Joey." Andy tugged his coat collar closer around his face. "I've come to see if there's any hope at stopping this thing."

"I don't think so." Joey returned to his semi-relaxed position as Matthew Broader took the floor.

"I was against striking last time." Broader slapped his hat against his thigh. "But the bank called in my loan today. The drought is taking my crops, and the infection is taking my cows. If we don't get an honest dollar for our milk, I'm going to lose my farm, and my children will be homeless."

"Is all that true?" Andy whispered, lifting his hat to run his hands through his hair, then squaring it firmly on his head. "There's no chance of stopping it, then. The only hope is negotiating a fair deal to hold them over until the government actually raises prices."

"Will your father do that?"

He gave him a side eye. That's what Joey thought. Andy sighed. "I really hoped my relationship with Amy would help."

"Where does that leave the two of you?" Not that it was his business. No, it was definitely his concern. Especially after the argument in his parents' yard this afternoon.

"I love her." Andy's words were choked. "You think your dad is going to give me permission to marry her with this hanging over us?"

No, but ... Understanding struck. "That's the real reason you're here. If there's a strike, you could lose Amy."

Andy didn't answer.

"Don't you dare do anything foolish, like run away with her." He couldn't believe he was saying this. "You want to destroy this town? That will do it."

"You don't have to tell me," Andy hissed back. "I've already thought of that."

"At least you're thinking." Unlike half this town.

"Not well. Amy is beside herself." Andy's voice faltered. "What am I supposed to do?"

Oh, he did not want to have this conversation. Did not want to mediate between his love-struck sister and their dad. Their mother and her dreams for her daughters. This town and the young love it could destroy. But as the middle child, that had always been his role, and now, not only the fate of his baby sister's heart stood on the line, but that of an entire town did too. Horsefeathers. Maybe even his own happiness was at stake.

Joey sighed. "I'll talk to Dad."

"What?" Hope raised Andy's volume and Joey shushed him.

"I can't promise anything, but if I spin it right, maybe I can work something out for you and Amy."

"I know we haven't always been friends—"

"You mean we've never been friends."

Andy grinned. "You were too easy to prank when we were school-age."

"Don't make me regret my offer."

"Thank you, Joey." Andy held out a hand. "I mean it."

"Yeah, yeah." But Joey shook his hand. "Better get out of here before they realize who you are."

After Joey watched the young man slip out the door, he leaned back against the wall, arms and ankles crossed once again. Why did he let himself get in these situations? How was he going to convince his father, with whom he could barely have a civil word these days, that the man should let his enemy's son marry his baby girl? If Amy was his daughter, Joey would never agree to it.

CHAPTER 12

Katy groomed Clover in the quiet of her barn late that night. Glenn snuffled in his feed bin. Nessa chewed her cud, her calf making suckling noises. Most dairy farmers didn't keep calves with their mothers longer than a couple days, but Lily kept them fully together for three months. The calf saved her from having an excess of milk when farmers often paid for her veterinary services in dairy products, at least until gardens came in and other produce was available.

Mr. Moore had paid her in hay today, as he had ever since she brought Clover home, and loaded it into her truck while she talked to Katy. Gratefully, the Moore's farmyard had been empty when she drove away since her mind had been churning ever since.

"It's curious, don't ya think, boy?" she whispered to the horse. "Now that I think on it, I reckon Mr. Moore knows more about your previous owner than he lets on, and I don't get the feelin' it's anything good." Like the milk strike business.

Clover switched his tail and rotated his ears.

"Ah, boy, you know somethin', too, eh? But I'm needing to coax it out of you like a certain emerald-eyed police officer." She smiled despite herself. His story today had cracked her defenses, and she wasn't all that sorry about it. Yes, she was wary—but hopeful he truly was one of the rare good men.

Clover stomped his hoof.

"Right. It's quite a quandary, Clover, boy." Katy worked through the horse's coarse mane with a comb, standing on a stool to reach. "Coming to a new country seems much less scary than lettin' Joey get close. I know in me head he is different from the other men, but is it enough?"

The rumble of a car brought Katy to the barn door. Clover whinnied and Glenn brayed. Katy clasped the comb tighter, its tines digging into her palm. Fergus Cormac had returned.

The man made his way to her in the dusky evening, sharply dressed in a perfectly tailored navy suit. Why did he insist on visiting at this time of night? Did he wish not to be seen visiting her? Maybe he didn't, if it was true that his father was killed, but something about Mr. Cormac's story didn't sit right.

"It is good to see you again, Miss Wells." Mr. Cormac doffed his bowler, too much charm in his tone.

"Mr. Cormac." Katy extended him no courtesy. Based on their noise, her animals seemed no more comfortable with his presence than she. "What brings you back?"

"I have word from your uncle."

That uneasy feeling churned stronger, but instead of retreating to Clover's side, she held her ground.

"I gave him your answer—that you'd willingly hand over the money, but that wasn't good enough for him, just as I warned. He crossed the Atlantic and is coming here."

Katy's head spun. All possibility that the problem would go away with Mr. Cormac's absence vanished. Instead, it had grown worse. Much, much worse.

"When he arrives, I can attempt a peaceful negotiation, but I doubt he'll have any of it."

Katy tucked her hands under her arms. "How long do I have until he gets here?"

"Days."

"I need to think." She kept her voice as strong as possible, though fear snaked through her. "Thank you for warning me, Mr. Cormac."

"Let me help you come up with a plan." He reached for her, but she stepped back. Clover smacked the ground with his hooves, and Glenn butted the door of his stall.

"Perhaps tomorrow." She needed him to leave. Needed space from him to think clearly and for her animals to regain their peace so she could as well.

"We don't have that much time." Mr. Cormac frowned. "Surely, you can see there are only a few options. Just handing over the money is no longer one of those. Have you thought about my offer? A marriage of—".

"Good evening, Mr. Cormac."

He huffed but retreated. "As you wish. I will return in the morning."

Katy sank to the ground as Mr. Cormac drove away, body trembling too much to hold her up. Nessa and Glenn peered at her over their stall doors. Clover waved his large head, pawing the ground, tail held aloft.

"Easy, boy." She went to him. Stroking his forelock with trembling fingers calmed her enough for one thought to flash in her mind. *Joey*. Because something about the whole situation seemed fishy, and Katy knew better than to trust a man to have her best interests in mind.

Except for Joey. After hearing his story today, she knew he would look out for her. Not because he was a policeman or even because she was his twin's friend, but because Joey Moore was a good man. A man she could trust. And right now, that's exactly the type of man she needed since her life and livelihood could depend on solving the riddle of Daideó's inheritance.

Joey snapped up his suspenders before answering the knock at his door. His small apartment kept him in town, which was advantageous as an officer and a volunteer firefighter. However, he rarely got personal visitors except for family members, and he'd already stopped by Lil's before the vote. She'd kicked him out, too upset over Mom's dinner ambush to talk to him.

Joey pushed away the personal thoughts as he flung open his door. "Katy?"

"Can we talk?" She gripped her medical bag as if wringing a chicken's neck and glanced over her shoulder. She wore no jacket over the light, short-sleeved dress, and her hair was tied up in a messy pile. He'd never seen her look this undone, and it scared him more than anything he'd faced before.

"Give me one minute." He hated leaving her on the step, but he wouldn't risk her reputation at this time of night. Instead, he left the front door open as he jogged into his bedroom for his vest and jacket and a spare coat for Katy. He snatched his hat and weapon on his way back to the door.

She hadn't moved.

"Tell me what's going on." He wrapped the coat around her shoulders, then cupped her elbow as he led them down the steps that ran along the outside of the building. She pulled free to wrap her arm around his, as if hanging on to keep from drowning.

"Fergus Cormac just paid me a visit." Her voice trembled as much as her body. If that man laid a hand on her …

He covered her fingers as they dug into his bicep and directed them down the sidewalk. They needed a private place to talk, and he knew just the place. "Can you start at the beginning? What exactly did Cormac tell you?"

She rambled as they walked, and Joey had to press close to her to catch every word beneath her strengthening accent. It brought back memories of their near-kiss, but he pushed them away. Now was not the time.

"Then I came right over to you." Katy's breath came in quick gasps as he settled her on a bench in the cemetery behind the church. Gas lamps cast an eerie glow, and the mild air held a cloying tension.

"I'm glad you did." He sat beside her, then squeezed her hand. Cormac's actions warned of some deeper plot that did not bode well for Katy's security. "We'll figure this out together."

She nodded. "I'm scared, Joey. Mr. Cormac—I don't like him. Something isn't right. I can't put me finger on it. I don't know if it's him as a person or his story or both. I don't know if I can trust what he's saying about me uncle. Would he really come all the way from Ireland to get me money? Is the money even real? The lawyer I contacted hasn't provided any information. If only I hadn't run away when I heard my uncle threaten to put me in that awful place, I might know the truth."

"You also might be in a workhouse. You did the right thing, running away. Your freedom is worth whatever money your grandfather left you."

"You truly believe that, don't you?"

"You know I do. With all my heart."

She slid closer to him, laying her head on his shoulder. He wrapped his arm around her, holding her tight and remembering the light in her eyes when she'd called him a good man earlier that day. It humbled him even as the desire to live up to her picture of him swelled his chest.

"Perhaps it's time I meet this Fergus Cormac." Joey finally broke the silence that hung between them.

"Och, perhaps it is, but …"

"What is it?"

She raised her head to look at him. "What if it makes it worse? I keep hoping this is all just idle threats. That none of it is real. What if your presence provokes them?"

Joey let the thought sink in before replying. "What is it that makes you believe that?"

"Right now they see me as a weak woman, but if I bring another man into the negotiations, won't that change their tactics?"

Possibly. Likely. Joey held in a sigh. "Can you tell me more about your uncle?"

"Uncle Patrick, he's Mother's brother—Daideó's son—but two men could not be more different. Where Daideó was patient and gentle, Uncle Patrick was harsh and loud. He liked his pints, and he did not like the agrarian life." She brushed the fabric of her skirt, though Joey saw no debris. "He worked in the wool factory, working his way up to foreman by the time I left. He was several years older than my mother and refused to acknowledge her as his sister after she was sent away."

"He seems like the type who would prefer to take your money the easy way."

"Precisely. Mr. Cormac's story about that being the reason Uncle Patrick wanted to send me to the laundry makes sense. If there truly is that much money. I can hardly believe that, though. Daideó was a generous man. One of my favorite memories of him was one spring during lambing season."

If only he could capture the joy that washed over her expression. If only he could make it so that she never need express fear again.

"Somehow, this little lamb got separated from her mother. It bleated and bleated until Daideó found it huddled in the crook of two rocks. He tucked the little thing under his arm and searched the herd until he found the ewe. Not until the pair were happily reconnected did he return to whatever it was that brought him to that farm, no matter his personal inconvenience."

Joey stayed quiet as she paused to gather herself.

"I'll never forget how he held that little lamb, the tenderness he showed. He gave of himself, but always in the present. I can't see him putting money away for later when it could have been put straight to use. He would have been more likely to give it away once it reached his hand. It was his way."

"I wouldn't be so sure about that." He tightened his arm about her shoulders. "You were his little lamb. He would have made sure you were safe if he couldn't be there. He knew he couldn't give money to you until you came of age, and he knew his son. Putting money aside for your independence would be one of the best gifts he could give you."

Tears shimmered in her eyes. "You think he did that?"

"For your sake, I hope he did."

"But I don't want the money, Joey. Not if it means Uncle Patrick is holding a grudge. Not if it's the reason I had to leave Ireland."

"I agree with you. But if it buys you your freedom?"

Katy wove her fingers together over and over. "You know, Mr. Cormac suggested a marriage of convenience. Do you think he could've manufactured a situation where he could force me to marry him? Why else come all the way from Ireland just for little ol' me? I've been gone for fourteen years."

His stomach churned at the thought. "The answer to that question may be the solution to the problem, and the only way we'll find out is if we talk to Cormac."

"We."

He pressed a knuckle under her chin so she would look at him. "We. No expectations. No strings."

Tears welled in her eyes, and his heart twisted. How he wished a kiss would show how cherished she was, but he'd made that mistake once already. Instead, he settled for resting his forehead against hers.

She shifted beneath his touch, her lips a hairsbreadth from his. He squeezed his eyes closed as she brushed the lightest of kisses across them. He dare not deepen the moment, so he cupped her cheek and pulled away.

Uncertainty shimmered in her eyes.

"When this is over,"—he ran his thumb over her cheek—"when there is no question of why, then I hope you'll let me kiss you again."

CHAPTER 13

From inside his car, Fergus Cormac stared through his binoculars at the couple sitting on the bench in the church cemetery. Shadows partially obscured them, but not enough to squelch the anger that surged through him. Caitlin "Katy" Wells had a beau.

Fourteen years he'd been waiting. At first, with hope that the pretty granddaughter of the local veterinarian would notice him. And then, when she'd fled, with a longing for her that had given birth to carefully constructed plans. Plans that were being wrecked before his very eyes. Bile rose in his throat as the intimate moment bloomed between Caitlin and the usurper. The policeman. He couldn't let him take— *Wait! Did she ... Did she just kiss him?*

No! He slammed his hand on the steering wheel. *No! No! No!*

He shouldn't have let three months go by, but things had turned out to be more complicated than expected with returning that boy to Ireland. He hadn't thought there a risk to leave Caitlin just a few weeks longer. Plus, he'd needed better leverage to get everything he wanted.

Those early years of hoping had been puppy love—he knew that, but when she'd disappeared, he hadn't anticipated the longing that erupted. He'd helped search for her, but they found no trace. After that, he'd tried calling on other girls, but none measured up to her. None had her kindness. Her raven hair. Her eyes like the sea.

He could never have been more grateful than when Father found her in London. That was the moment Fergus knew he would marry Caitlin Wells. He'd been at university for a couple years, but he would have quit for her, lived where she lived. He could have made her happy. Only, Caitlin had disappeared again before he could propose.

For years after, he'd helped his father try to find her. They'd scoured England, then the Continent. Then Patrick Wells pursued declaring his niece dead. But Fergus wouldn't give up. He knew she wasn't dead. She couldn't be because she was meant to be Fergus's wife. He just had to find her.

When he'd spotted her name on that Cornell student list four years ago, all the hope he'd built up turned into a driving desire. Patrick Wells demanded proof of life. He wanted the money Caitlin's grandfather had left her. Fergus didn't care about the money, but he wouldn't let Patrick destroy his dream of marrying Caitlin. Fergus prepared to move to America to find Caitlin and protect her, but then his mom grew ill, he and his father discovered the truth about the money, and Father was murdered.

The policeman tucked Fergus' Caitlin under his arm and directed her back into town. No, Fergus wouldn't let anything or anyone come between him and Caitlin. He wouldn't allow his father's death to be for nothing. Patrick Wells had cost him too much already, and nothing, not even a policeman, would stand in Fergus' way.

The moving pieces were coming together. He wouldn't believe the past months of delay were in vain. Since it appeared he would need to apply pressure to convince Caitlin to agree to marry him, he would do so. Then she and Fergus would take her money and disappear so no one, not this policeman or the ones looking for Fergus in Ireland, would ever find them.

CHAPTER 14

Wednesday, May 18

Five days of heightened stress had Katy wondering if she'd aged years in the same span of time. Perhaps this was why Daideó had always mentioned his sore back and creaky knees. She gritted her teeth at just such a pain as she climbed the two steps to her back door.

Each of the past five days had seen another cow come down with the mastitis infection—never had she seen so many cases on so many different farms—and each day, tempers grew hotter at the strike site. She worried for Joey's safety as he and his few fellow policemen attempted to keep things peaceful. She worried for Lily as the pressure mounted on her friend to marry before her little sister, who was practically engaged. She worried for the Broaders who could lose their farm any day now. And she worried for her patients. Couldn't she stop the infections before it cost a life? She needed that new antibiotic.

The only relief she got was her daily ride on Clover. The big horse didn't care to gallop, or even canter. A nice trot to check on the fields was more to his liking, and it appeared that what hay there was would be ready to cut any day now, which meant food for her animals for at least a little while longer.

She shivered as a cool breeze followed her into the house. After last week's warm snap, spring clung on, so as not to give in to summer. The sun, however, had other plans. It warmed the dry ground—ground so thirsty that watering her seeds by hand might not be enough. Katy's muscles ached from the effort. Her hands were soft from the balm she continually rubbed into the cow udders. Her jaw was stiff from clenching it whenever night came for fear Fergus Cormac or her uncle would appear on her property.

Above all, she was tired. Katy set her medical bag on the table and sank into a hardback chair, resting her elbows on the table's surface, head in her hands. Food and coffee would help. She pushed to her feet and stoked the fire, setting the kettle on the woodstove. Taking cheese from the icebox, she cut several slices to go with the dried venison a farmer had given her this morning.

A car pulling into her drive interrupted a yawn. She peered out the kitchen window but couldn't see who it was. She wasn't up for visitors—especially Mr. Cormac. Right now, she didn't even have the energy for Joey. She might embarrass herself and ask for a hug. Or worse, a kiss.

Her cheeks heated at the memory of her brazenness in kissing Joey last week. She tried for years to not be like her mother, and there she'd gone and kissed a man. Maybe she deserved to be in a Magdalene Laundry. The thought sent a shiver down her spine.

At a knock on her back door, she jumped, sending the kitchen knife sailing out of her hand. It clattered to the ground, sounding very much like her jangling nerves.

The knock came again, and she tossed the knife into the wash basin as she headed for the door. Pulling it open, she found Irvin Wallace on her back step.

"What's wrong?" She stared at the farmer, a bulge of tobacco in his lower lip.

"The infection." He said it with a sneer, and Katy fought back the feelings of inadequacy. A male veterinarian would have equal trouble fighting this as she did. Right?

"Let me get my medical bag." She turned back inside only for the sound of Mr. Wallace's work boots to follow her. "You can wait there. I'll only be—"

"I ain't going nowhere." The man slammed the door, blocking her way out. His scraggly beard jutted from his chin and his eyes gleamed with a calculating meanness. "We have business to discuss."

"I don't believe we do." She backed up to the table, her fingers grasping at the worn edge. If only she'd left that knife here rather than putting it in the wash basin.

"You are a difficult woman to pin down, Dr. Wells." He spit her title at the floor along with a stream of tobacco juice. "I come to offer you a deal."

"A deal for what?" She eased around the table to keep it between them.

"You ain't welcome in my town. A woman doctor, even to animals." He spit again, but it only punctuated the anger that simmered under his gray-toned skin. "I finally found a way to get rid of you for good."

"How?" Her imagination attempted to take flight, but she wrestled it back to earth. "Why?"

"It's been gnawin' at me that you short-changed me for my horse when I was in a bad situation, but I hear you're comin' into some money. Pay me what it's worth, and I won't call you a horse thief."

"You signed a receipt. Clover is mine, free and clear."

"You think that matters? With your reputation—or the one you'll have when I'm done? I hear you were a flirtatious child, just like your mother. You needed discipline, proved by the fact you ran away and now live here alone like a harlot."

Katy's cheeks flamed. There were only a few people who would have told him that, and none of them were Joey.

"How many men come in and out of your house? Hmm?" His sneer had Katy easing toward her door.

"What do ya want, Mr. Wallace? Besides money I don't have."

"I want you to leave town so I can bring in my own animal doctor. Before you go, I'll take a plate of cheese and coffee." He nodded at the food on her counter. "It's all a woman is good for. Well. Almost all."

Horrible thoughts threatened to undo her, but Katy nabbed her medical bag. "Then we have nothing more to discuss." Katy darted for the door, leaving the disgusting man alone in her house.

"It's the right thing to do, Dad." Joey leaned against the brick wall that surrounded the Booths' dairy processing building. The sun beat down, warmer than it had been the last five days of standing here. Beat down and gave him a headache. He resisted the urge to rub the ache away.

"My daughter is not a negotiating tool." Dad's solid stance attempted to mask the weariness beneath. The man had been going non-stop for five days, taking care of his sick cows while leading the strike. Exhaustion did not make for good decisions, but Joey wasn't above using it to get his dad to agree to something he wouldn't otherwise.

Joey shrugged to appear as nonchalant about the matter as possible. "You know Amy loves Andy and Andy loves Amy."

"I know nothing of the kind."

"I do. Andy is lovesick and will do anything for her."

Dad looked as though he'd swallowed a cup of dirt. "And Amy?"

"Considering how mad she was when she heard Mom wants Lily to marry Andy instead? Yeah, she is in love with him." And as much as Joey would like his twin safe and settled, that was a battle for a different day. Right now, he needed to see to his youngest sister's happiness.

Dad frowned. "Is Booth willing to negotiate a truce?"

Ah, the real sticking point.

"Andy is, and I think he can convince his father to put his son's happiness before profit."

His dad grunted. "If my little girl is happy, I'll talk to Andy." Success, though Dad would have put up a much bigger fight if he wasn't even half as tired.

Joey squeezed Dad's shoulder, then spotted Katy weaving through the crowd of farmers blocking the road to the dairy. "I'll be right back."

Wow, he'd missed her. Who was he to roll his eyes at Andy's eagerness when he had to restrain his feet from jogging to meet Katy? Excitement turned to worry when he saw her face.

"He's here, Joey." Katy greeted him, her face pale and drawn.

Joey took her elbow and pulled her away from nosy eyes and ears. "Cormac?"

"My uncle. I'm sure of it. I haven't seen him, but how else would Mr. Wallace know so much about my past? Things only Uncle would know—well, and you, but I know you wouldn't say a word."

"Take a breath." He rubbed his neck to keep from rubbing her arms. This wasn't the place to give even a hint of closeness. The agitation in these farmers could turn an innocent gesture into fuel. "What's this about Irvin Wallace? He's been here all day."

"I left him in me house. He's trying to extort money from me for Clover, and he wants me to leave town so he can bring in his own veterinarian. I can only imagine what that means. What can another doctor do that I cannot? Could he have access to the medicine I'd desperately like to use?"

"Katy, I don't follow." He loved her accent, but not when she got excitable that he couldn't understand her.

"I cannot just give him what he wants. He's so crude and mean. If I give him the money, I lose any leverage."

"Extortion is illegal. But either way, it's your word against his."

"And I'm a woman." She squeezed her eyes shut, her jaw hard as stone. "I just need someone to help me get him out of my house."

Joey looked back at the farmers, gauging whether he could leave and be back before anyone could miss him. They jostled and pushed on another, then he spotted a face or two he didn't recognize. Horsefeathers. "Katy, I can't leave my post. Go over to Lily's until later this afternoon. It's the best I can do right now."

"I wouldn't take you away from your job." She took a step back. "I'll manage."

"No, no." He ached to pull her closer, undo the separation duty put between them. "Wait for me, please."

"I know, Joey." She gave him a distant smile. "Stay safe."

"Katy."

But she'd disappeared into the crowd. Joey clamped down on the growl vibrating in his throat. He couldn't leave his post, could he? If the farmers destroyed the Booths' property, would the fault be his? How had it come to this? Since when did standing between these farmers and a greedy plant owner trump ensuring a vulnerable woman's safety—a woman he cared about? This wasn't why he became a policeman. This wasn't helping people.

It wasn't helping Katy. He'd just let her walk away to face her problems on her own. Maybe he really was just like his father. Because putting his job before Katy felt like the biggest mistake of his life.

She shouldn't have gone to see Joey. Katy couldn't have asked him to sacrifice his job for her, even if a part of her hoped he'd do just that. It wasn't fair. Not to any of them. And she sure wasn't bringing Lily into this. She wouldn't be the reason her friend got hurt. No. She needed to figure this out on her own.

Clear of the moving mass of farmers, Katy rounded the corner to the street where she'd left her truck, and her steps faltered. Fergus Cormac leaned against it. He was not someone she wished to deal with right now. Especially since he was the only other person who could possibly have told Mr. Wallace all those details. But how could even he know everything?

Mr. Cormac straightened as she approached. "He's here."

Her stomach dropped. She was right—Uncle Patrick was the source.

"We can figure this out together. I'm here for you. Whatever you need."

Katy tucked her hands under her arms. Why couldn't Joey have used those exact words?

"My offer stands, Caitlin. Marry me, and your uncle won't be able to touch you."

She shivered and backed away as Mr. Cormac reached for her. "I'm not ready to go that far."

"You might not have a choice." Why did that sound like a threat?

"There's always a choice. I've been making them since I ran away at twelve years old."

"You'd run again?" He shook his hands as if he had her neck clasped between them. "Instead of marrying me?"

"Because I'd be trading one cage for another."

Mr. Cormac flug his arms wide. "Marriage is not a cage."

"It is if there isn't love."

"Love would grow." He paced a step either way before snagging her hands. "Caitlin, I already love you."

She froze. "What did you say?"

"I've loved you since the first day I saw you. You've never been far from my thoughts. Now I have the chance to save you. Let me, please."

Katy tugged her hands away and cast about for something solid— someone other than Mr Cormac—to hold her up. First, Mr. Wallace wanted her money, then Joey couldn't help her, and now Mr. Cormac wanted to marry her this instant—all in a single day?

A grin perked his lips. "Your silence is not a *no*."

But it was. She squared her shoulders. "I am not that desperate."

"Desperate? My offer has nothing to do with desperation, but rather with protection. By marrying me, I would stand between you and your uncle. He couldn't get the land or the money away from us. We would have it together. We could go anywhere together. Do anything together. Please say yes. We can go to the preacher right now."

Panic closed around her throat, silencing any attempt at cutting him off.

"I know your uncle." Mr. Cormac's insistence grew in firmness as he again closed the distance between them. "I'm the only way to stop him. If the money is ours, not just yours, he can't take it by locking you up. He can't hurt you because he'd have to go through me. See, it makes all the sense." He touched her arm. "Marry me, Caitlin Wells."

Hearing her laundry-given name, her feet unglued and she ran. Tears blinded her eyes, but she needed to get alone. To think without the pressure of someone putting ideas in her head. To discern if marriage was truly her only way to escape these threats. Because there was only one man she wanted to stand between her and her uncle, between Irvin Wallace and his blackmail.

And it wasn't Fergus Cormac.

CHAPTER 15

Joey paced uneasily as the number of farmers surged, including the faces he didn't recognize. His chief arrived minutes after Katy left, removing any chance of chasing after her. Rumors circulated that Waukesha County had brought in the National Guard, which had used tear gas and bayonets on the men striking outside Milwaukee. It left everyone here, farmers and policemen alike, skittish, but Joey's unease had more to do with how he'd left things with Katy.

He rubbed the back of his neck as he gauged how long until milking time. If pattern held, the farmers would disperse soon to tend their cows, ending today's standoff.

Normally, Eagle's farmers cooled their milk in ponds until after the morning milking, but those wishing to cross the strike line had been spotted delivering their supply of milk after dark instead. Some dairies collected the milk by sending a truck from farm to farm, but Booth hadn't added that service—good in this case because that was one less truck to worry about getting accosted. Then again, perhaps adding the service—for free instead of for the usual fee—could be part of the negotiation Andy and Dad were conducting right now. One could hope, right?

At a commotion among the farmers, Joey straightened and rested his hand on his revolver. He scanned the crowd for the cause, but most of the farmers were looking behind Joey. He turned in time to see one of Booth's trucks jostling its way toward the gate.

Joey joined the three other officers—all the members of Eagle's police force—and their chief in putting themselves between the crowd and the truck. It was a show. A reminder. A plea to keep things civil. Otherwise, would the policemen be forced to open fire on neighbors and family members to defend the dairy? Trepidation snaked up Joey's spine like poison ivy.

The truck turned around before stopping within the yard, its bed facing toward the crowd. Andy emerged from the driver's side, and the murmuring crowd grew louder. He circled the truck, then helped someone out from the passenger side. No. *No, no no.* What was Andy thinking, bringing Amy here? How could they protect her if the crowd turned violent?

Andy helped Amy into the truck bed, then climbed up after her. He waved his arms. The clamoring drowned out his words. The confidence in Amy's expression spurred Joey to silence the crowd with a whistle. Andy and their dad had reached a deal.

Andy gave him the subtlest of nods, then addressed the farmers. "I come with a truce. Before anyone gets hurt or business relations become too soured, it's time to sit at the table and talk. Mr. Moore and I have already begun."

Joey tried to catch Amy's eye as Andy grasped her hand. She didn't look at him. She had eyes only for Andy. That was good, wasn't it? Joey wished nothing but happiness for his sister, but was this truly the only way? She had feelings for him, but starting a relationship with a strike between them suddenly seemed a bad idea. Had he done right by helping broker the relationship? Should he have done more to protect his sister?

Andy raised his and Amy's clasped hands. "As a sign of good faith and a promise of negotiations to come, Amy Moore and I would like to announce our engagement."

One of the farmers shouted at Dad, who'd appeared on the sidelines. "You agreed to this, Moore?"

"You have daughters. See that look on her face?" Dad crossed his arms. "We're going to make this work."

Heaven help him, he'd gotten this wrong. This wasn't the answer. Hinging everything on the marriage of two young people? Yes, they seemed to love one another, but to wed two enemy families? When the heads of both would prefer to duel it out? Panic wrapped around his throat.

"A wedding in the family, eh?" Irvin Wallace landed a hand on Joey's shoulder, making him flinch. When did he get here? And where was Katy? "How's that other sister of yours feel about getting passed over? I'd think she would be the one your father used to tie him to that dairy shark."

"Leave my sister out of it." Joey glared at him, barely catching himself from adding Katy's name to his demand.

Wallace spat a stream of tobacco. "Your father made your sisters fair game with this stunt. Wonder what he'd offer for the older one. World peace?"

Joey pulled back a fist only to have someone grab his arm before he could deliver a blow to the farmer's nose.

"Not worth it, Moore." Mr. Broader tugged him back. "Crowd's dispersing."

Wallace laughed. "Maybe stop by the vet. She'll—"

"That's enough!" Mr. Broader pushed Wallace into the crowd.

The farmers moved around Joey for a moment before parting as the chief approached. The lean man waved a paper. "Thirty farmers were injured in Shawano County three days ago. Forty or so were arrested in Milwaukee County two days ago. And the report just came in, National Guardsmen took on three hundred picketers in Waukesha County today."

Joey fought off the nausea. "The rumors were true, then?"

"Worse. It was a battle like my father—a Union soldier—muttered about in his dreams. Bombs, bayonets, like they were rushing Missionary Ridge all over again. Between you and me, we're not equipped for this, but I don't want to bring in the Guard—not at the risk of injuring or killing our farmers. Although, we might not have a choice."

Joey planted his hands on his belt. "Why tell me, sir?"

"Because you have your father's ear. Maybe he'll listen to you. These negotiations—maybe something good will come of them. Something that will save people. But I worry." Chief squinted toward the setting sun. "If the farmers see your sisters as bargaining chips, they might try to leverage your twin to get your father to make higher demands. I hope I'm wrong, but keep an eye on her."

No one would force negotiations to go their way by using his sisters, would they? Yet, wasn't that exactly what they'd done to Amy? She might be a willing participant, but Lily would never be. Worst case scenarios swirled in Joey's head as he jogged to his car. First he'd deliver the warning to Lily—check whether Katy had taken refuge there as he'd asked— then he could turn his full attention to Katy's safety.

He found his twin in the corral behind her dog barn, two hanging lanterns illuminating the twilight. Lined up in front of her were five dogs-in-training, including her own curly-coated one. Lily's eyes, identical to his, lit up when she spotted him. The dogs—except hers, of course—broke rank, barking as they leapt up on the fence to greet him. Her own dog wagged his tail in the dirt as he watched Joey's approach with affectionate brown eyes.

"This group is hard-headed." Lily released her own dog with a slight move of her hand. The dog trotted to the fence and nosed between the others to reach Joey's outstretched hand. "At this rate, it's going to take me an extra week to get them to listen well enough to practice retrieving out at the pond."

"It's never taken you longer than three weeks to get a dog to listen off his lead." Joey rubbed the coarse, curly fur of his twin's dog. The other dogs wandered toward the water trough or followed other smells within the corral.

She laughed. "True, and in that case, it was only because I ran out of venison jerky. That particular dog wouldn't obey for any other reward." She paused for only a moment. "But that's not why you're here. What's wrong? The strike ... is there news?"

Joey scratched his chin. That was the problem with having a twin—they could read each other better than anyone else ever could. "Amy's engaged." He spit out that news first.

"We knew that was coming."

"Are you okay with it? Her getting married when you're not."

Lily fingered the cuff of her farm coat and her dog left Joey to sit on her foot. "Doesn't feel good if I think of it that way—as though I'm last to be chosen for a game—but would I trade my privacy here at the farmhouse for a business arrangement? No. I'll get through the wedding and stop my ears to all the gossip, but not before I threaten Mom with not helping her plan anything unless she promises not to bring up one more man's name. None of them suit."

That was all well and good, but ... "You sure you're okay being alone here?"

"We've been over this, Joey. This is my home. I'll be fine. I promise. Once the wedding is over, no one will remember you and I prefer to remain unmarried."

Joey forced himself to take an even breath. If he and Katy became an item, Lily would be the lone unattached member of the Moore household. Could he really do that to his twin? The sibling with whom he shared the closest bond? Especially since his relationship was with her dearest friend?

"Is there something else? You seem troubled." Her voice was quiet, inviting him to share.

"There's a possibility of things turning personal."

"With the strike? I'm not surprised, which is why I'm staying away from it. I left Dad's dairy business for a reason, and I don't intend to get dragged back in."

"The chief warned me that Amy's involvement may mean you don't have a choice. You'll tell us if you feel your safety is in danger, right?"

"Mm." She studied him with an eye trained toward assessing behavior, albeit canine behavior. "Are you sure that's the something else?"

No. "Only a long day guarding the strike line, that's all." He offered a tired smile, hoping it would fend off further questions. He'd tell his twin eventually. Right now, his priority was to make sure Katy was safe.

As darkness fell, Katy approached her house cautiously. There were no other cars in her yard, so she hoped that meant her house was now empty. No more surprise visitors. No more unwelcome suggestions. No more pressure to do something she had no interest in doing. Like get married. Or leave town.

The door was unlocked, but a quick search with her bag held as a weapon assured her the house was indeed empty. Katy let out the breath she'd been holding and washed up. She'd avoided coming home for as long as she could, visiting patients that didn't really need an extra visit, but she couldn't stay away forever. Though she didn't hold out much hope that night would keep Mr. Cormac from visiting, perhaps Joey would come by first.

Shrugging a coat over her cotton dress, Katy carried a lantern to the barn for evening chores. Getting Nessa and her calf settled took no time at all. She'd miss having the gangly little animal around, but she couldn't afford to feed two cows once the calf stopped drinking her mother's milk.

Glenn took a bit more time. Her usually sweet donkey seemed out of sorts, digging in his heels as she directed him to his stall. She asked him whatever could be the matter, but he merely brayed his displeasure. So she left him tied in the aisle while she descended to her root cellar for two of the last carrots from last year's harvest. One did the trick, and Glenn was tucked in for the night.

The other carrot, Katy held out for Clover once she secured him in the aisle for his nightly grooming, but he refused it.

"Right, my boy. Are you not feelin' well either?" She tucked the carrot in her pocket before running her hands over Clover's rippling muscles. Everything felt fine except for the tension.

Clover stomped his hoof and Glenn brayed

Tingling slipped down Katy's spine.

"About my deal, Dr. Wells." Irvin Wallace stood in the barn door-way. *Dear Father of Mercy.*

"I don't have anything to give you." She faced him. "I haven't seen a will to even know if I have any money."

Mr. Wallace stalked closer. Clover rose on his hind legs as far as his lead would allow. Katy backed into the dangerous place between the agitated horse and one of the beams to which he was secured.

"Stop!" The command came from Fergus Cormac, not Joey, and he leveled a pistol at Mr. Wallace. Glenn kicked in his stall. First came the rattle of tin, then the *sploosh* of water.

The farmer spun on Mr. Cormac. "Who are you?"

"Do you have the will?" Katy blurted out the question, not waiting to hear how Mr. Cormac answered Mr. Wallace's question.

"I ain't looking for trouble." Mr. Wallace eyed the pistol. "You can take the girl and go. I'll sell her animals for the money I want."

Father God ... This was getting out of hand. "Can we take a breath? Find a way to compromise so everyone is happy?" So her animals didn't pay the price. They were as unnerved by the presence of these men as she was.

"Compromise?" Mr. Wallace glared at her from where he'd backed himself against the beam between Nessa's and Glenn's stalls. "I came for what's mine."

"I can't let you have it." Mr. Cormac, who'd been inching closer to Katy, pulled back the hammer on his pistol.

"Don't!" Uncontrollable panic squeezed Katy's throat. If his shot went wide, he'd hurt Glenn or Nessa or the calf.

"I'm trying to protect you, Caitlin," he hissed.

Dark spots crowded her vision. "Shooting him isn't the answer. Fergus, please." Panicking wasn't the answer either. "If you promise to leave me alone, Mr. Wallace, you can have it. If there even is any money. I don't want it. I haven't needed it. I have the best part of Daideó's legacy, and I'd prefer my independence than being manipulated, used, or threatened over material comfort."

"What are you thinking?" Mr. Cormac waved the gun, a wild look in his eyes. "We need that money. We need it to make a life together. You and me. It will give us our chance to start over. Without all this interference."

Clarity cut through her fear. Fergus Cormac had turned her into an item of obsession. The money, the land, his offer of help—none of it had nothing to do with him honestly desiring the best for her. Was Uncle Patrick actually on his way to Wisconsin? Or was that only Mr. Cormac's deception so he could claim her as his own?

She spoke quietly, as if soothing a bull she needed to tend. "Mr. Cormac, Fergus, there is no *we.*"

Mr. Wallace bellowed a laugh, shattering her attempt at calming the situation. "This is rich! You want a woman like her?"

"I love her." Mr. Cormac aimed his pistol at Mr. Wallace's chest.

CHAPTER 16

Joey froze outside the barn door. *He loves her?*

The words felt like a knife to the stomach, but he pushed it away to focus on Katy's safety. When he'd seen the extra cars in Katy's yard and didn't find her in the house, the barn was his second stop. Gun out of sight at his side, he eased the door aside, ready for whatever he would find.

Except this.

It took only the space of a blink to take in the situation. Katy stood near Clover, her back to the table, nearly shrinking into herself. Wallace leaned against the stalls opposite her as if this barn were his. And in the middle, a man not much older than himself spun at Joey's entrance, revealing a pistol in his right hand.

The next blink had Joey diving to the ground as the gun discharged, sending a bullet flying over his head.

What the ...?

Joey rolled and scrambled to press his back against the outside of the barn. How was he going to get Katy out of there? He tried to peek around the doorjamb to line up a shot, only to jerk back as the man fired another round out the door.

He slammed back against the wall, but Katy's cry galvanized him. He had to get inside.

"I have the girl," called the man he didn't recognize. "Throw your gun on the ground, put your hands where I can see them, and get in here."

That was one way to get into the barn. *God, protect her.*

"First, let her go." The man wouldn't go for it, but Joey had to try.

"I'll put a bullet in her."

"Okay, wait. Here I come." Joey unbuckled his holster, folded it so the gun could be easily retrieved, and tossed it inside.

"Slowly now."

Joey obeyed, hands raised beside his head. His first glance was for Katy. She stood flush against the unknown man's chest, his left arm around her middle, his right pressing the pistol behind her ear. Joey's stomach churned. He met her eyes. Fear and relief and a myriad of questions swam in the tears she tried to blink away.

Clover bucked against his restraints, slamming his humongous hooves in the dirt. Glenn kicked at his stall, eliciting not a few choice words from Irvin Wallace. And Nessa pressed into a far corner, the whites of her eyes reflecting the lantern light.

Joey squared his shoulders if only to project a confidence he didn't feel. "Are you Fergus Cormac?"

The man twitched, revealing Joey's guess was correct.

"Why did you have to interfere?" Cormac adjusted his hold on Katy, moving her away from the wild gelding.

Joey looked to Wallace, who'd just kicked at Glenn's stall door. "What are you doing here?"

"Who cares about him?" Panic edged Cormac's voice. Not good, especially while pointing a gun to Katy's head. "How dare you try to steal Caitlin when I've waited for her, pursued her, my entire life?"

Joey let out a slow, steadying breath. Rushing Cormac would not get Katy to safety.

"Fergus." Katy's gaze dug into Joey. "Tell him what you want, and he'll leave."

"What I want?" Cormac spoke through clenched teeth. "I want to know why you let this man come to your house, why you've seduced him"—he gave her a shake—"when you're supposed to be with me."

"I'm not—"

"She's not sure what you mean." Joey spoke over the animals' chaotic noise and shot Katy a meaningful look. For now, they had to go along with Cormac, not antagonize him with the truth.

"Right." Katy gave a subtle nod. "Joey is the brother of my friend. He's merely helping me … as a brother would."

"I saw you kiss him!"

Red bloomed on Katy's cheeks, and heat flared up Joey's neck.

Wallace bellowed a laugh that ended in a string of swear words when Glenn's square teeth chomped at the back of his coat.

"So I ask again …" Cormac pressed the gun into Katy's neck, making her wince as he directed the question at Joey. "What is your purpose here?"

No fooling this man, which meant it was time for the full truth. Joey peeled back his jacket to reveal the badge pinned on his vest. "I'm Officer Joey Moore of the Eagle police."

"I know!" Cormac thundered.

Katy whimpered, sending a knife into Joey's heart and Clover into a fresh flurry of fighting against his ties. The harness would already be digging into the tender skin around the gelding's face. It was only a matter of time before he broke the leads or splintered the beams holding him in place.

Too many innocents in this room of volatile men. This needed to end. Now.

Joey infused every bit of authority into his next sentence. "Then you need to let Dr. Wells go and come in with me."

Mr. Cormac bent to Katy's ear, his hot breath singeing her skin. "What are you doing associating with a cop? They're the type your uncle would have used to send you to the workhouse."

Mr. Wallace folded his arms across his filthy overalls. "You said she kissed him, right? Ain't that mean she used her wiles to get a cop in her corner?"

Katy gaped. Was that what these men thought of her?

Cormac spun Katy so that she faced him, her equilibrium rocking like water in a pail. "I can't believe you would betray me like that!"

"She's a woman." Wallace snorted. "What do you expect?"

"She's my woman." Fergus Cormac tightened his grip on Katy's arm. "And I'm not about to give her up. To either of you."

Every inch of Katy trembled. She squeezed her hands into tight fists, then flexed her fingers. Squeeze. Release. Squeeze. Release. The action paired with her breathing, clearing her mind.

"No one is trying to take her away from you, Cormac." Joey spoke calmly, with the authority that came from being a policeman. She couldn't see him now that she faced Mr. Cormac but latched onto his presence. Strength and clarity built into a resolve to stand up to these men.

"I ain't needing another woman," Mr. Wallace said, timing his words with what sounded like another spit. "I want her money."

Seconds slowed as Mr. Cormac removed the gun from her neck, and her gaze followed its aim to Mr. Wallace's chest. Joey—hero that he was—leapt between the men before Mr. Cormac could fire. Katy's heart stopped, waiting for the gunfire, for Joey to drop to the ground, dead.

Not on her life.

She pushed Mr. Cormac's shooting arm into the air. Deafening sound exploded from the gun. Her animals went wild against their confines. The bullet hit the ceiling, showering her with bits of wood. Mr. Cormac pulled her back toward him, the motion bringing back a specific memory.

With Joey's voice in her head, she inverted his instructions, letting the backward momentum carry her toward Mr. Cormac, and put all her weight into landing her heel on his foot. The man released a cry that she cut short with an elbow to his stomach. Then she spun to face him, planting a right hook in the man's nose.

Mr. Cormac dropped the gun as he pressed his hands to his face, blood dripping through his fingers. Pain shot through hers, and she grasped her hand.

Joey appeared, grabbing the gun as he reached for her, nearly spinning her as he pushed her behind him and out of the way of Clover's hooves. In the next moment, he had a gun in each hand, aiming at both Mr. Cormac and Mr. Wallace.

It happened so fast, Katy scrambled for breath, for stability. She leaned a hand, then a forehead, against Joey's back. Cold and heat whirled inside. Nausea twisted her belly.

"Your uncle was right about you." Cormac spat blood as he glared at her around Joey's torso. "Too bad he's dead, or I'd have delivered you to him myself."

"That's enough," Joey ordered. "Katy, do you have rope?"

Rope. Rope?

"I'll get it." Katy reached for Clover, who backed away as far as his lead would allow, the whites of his eyes showing as brightly as hers must have. Tears came as she reached for his halter. Underneath the leather, Clover's dark skin showed streaks of raw red where the straps had burned him.

"Katy." Joey's warning came through the haze, but she ignored it. Unhooking the lead, she turned Clover's head and sent him out the back door into the corral. His galloping hooves echoed the pounding in her heart. If only she could climb onto his back and let the fear melt away in an all out run. But she couldn't. She needed rope.

Fresh air filled her lungs as she reached the covered milking parlor behind the barn. She kept rope there as well as in the tack room, a room she couldn't get to, seeing as how the men blocked her way. Her fingers shook around the prickly straw that made up the rope, the feeling reminding her that she still lived and that she was still free.

Katy left Clover in the corral and moved back through the barn, stumbling to a stop within the shadows at Fergus Cormac's hate-filled words. "She won't have you, either, copper. She's a rotten woman, running every chance she gets."

A rotten woman.

She leaned against the back stall, hand pressing her throat.

"Then why did you want her so much?" Disgust laced Joey's words. "If you love someone like you claim, you'd be willing to sacrifice anything for them."

"I came to America for her," Cormac shouted.

"Uh-huh. Back to your knees. I'm placing you under arrest."

"For what?"

"Attempted murder, attempted kidnapping … need I go on?"

Mr. Cormac spat out a string of lilting Irish swear words. "If she had just come with me when I asked, this wouldn't be happening."

"Don't you dare blame someone else for your actions." Anger, hot and lethal, spewed from Joey. "Especially Katy Wells. Your actions are your responsibility. Yours alone and now you will pay for them."

"Moore, you're in love with her." Mr. Wallace laughed.

Joey loved her?

Joey. The handsomest man in Eagle. The one every girl fawned over. He *loved* her?

Flashing through her mind came the image of him putting himself between her and the bleeding Mr. Cormac, of him advocating for her to his father.

He loved *her.* Not any of the other women he could pick. Her. Katy Wells. Irish immigrant. Orphan. With a reputation fit only for a Magdalene Laundry.

Joey loved her.

"Both of you are complete saps." Mr. Wallace might not be referring to her, but he might as well have included her in the thought. She felt like a sap. A very happy sap. Because she returned Joey's feelings more than she liked to admit.

"Don't get on your high horse, Wallace. I'm placing you under arrest next. Extortion is illegal." Glenn added a solid *thwack* against his stall to accent Joey's words.

Now was the moment to stop this conversation from going further without revealing how much of it she'd overheard. Katy infused cheeriness into her tone as she entered the lantern light. "Here's the rope."

Joey quickly secured Mr. Cormac's hands, then Mr. Wallace's, seating them on the floor against the wall across from the stalls. Opposite them, Joey leaned against the beam between Nessa's and Glenn's stalls where Mr. Wallace had been. Katy stayed by his side, rubbing Glenn's little donkey head to comfort both herself and him. She was more than content to let Joey handle the situation.

How odd that a man could make her feel that way. Daideó and Joey's own grandfather were the only ones to ever come close to giving her a sense of security. Perhaps Joey had inherited some of his grandfather's ways—took after his mother's father rather than his own.

Joey turned her away from the other men and lowered his voice. "There might not be any money, any inheritance. Did you hear Cormac's slip? According to him, your uncle is dead. He may have manufactured the whole story just to scare you into marrying him."

Her heart twisted at the thought. Look where greed had brought Mr. Cormac and Mr. Wallace. What it may have cost her uncle. Why should she waste another moment worrying over this inheritance? Hadn't Joey told her how much he valued caring for a loved one over material things?

"What do I need with an inheritance in Ireland? This is my home now. We will be just fine, *mo mhuirnin*." My darling. She touched her lips as the endearment slipped out.

His gaze heated, and she knew he would have kissed her had the other two men not been sitting behind her.

CHAPTER 17

Thursday, May 19

The strike was over.

Joey breathed a sigh of relief as the chief delivered the news to the officers gathered in the police station. The governor of Wisconsin had agreed to form a committee run by dairy farmers in order to find a solution. However, Joey couldn't help but wonder if the governor's action would be enough to solve the problem.

For now, he needed to prepare a prisoner for transport.

Amy and Andy planned to spearhead the peace talks in Eagle, garnering goodwill as they focused the town on their October wedding. Probably good that Amy was the sister who chose the limelight. Lily would have run the other direction. As it was, Lily probably wouldn't show herself much these next few months.

Entering a back cell of the jail, Joey ignored the hatred pouring from Fergus Cormac as he secured him in a pair of handcuffs. Chief desired nothing to do with a case involving a foreigner, especially one wanted for questioning in the death of one Patrick Wells, and Joey didn't mind getting the man out of Eagle. Maybe Cormac would get shipped right back to Ireland and, at minimum, refused future reentry into the United States. Frankly, having the man in a Wisconsin jail seemed too close for comfort.

As it was, rumor abounded over why the Wallace family had deserted their farm overnight. Chief had given the farmer a choice—go through the process of a blackmail charge or quietly leave town. Perhaps the bank's latest foreclosure notices had also helped them make a decision.

The Broaders, on the other hand, were the recipients of the town's generosity. Farmers donated the money from that morning's milk delivery to their family and, rumor was, Andy added a bonus payment for them. Joey wished he could have helped in some way, but he needed to deliver Fergus Cormac to the sheriff's department.

He led the man through the office and out to his police car parked in front of the building. As much as he couldn't wait to send Cormac out of town, part of him strained to be with Katy. She'd insisted on going alone to meet with a lawyer outside of Milwaukee today. He'd sensed she needed to face her past, work through the legalities of her grandfather's death, and he would only get in the way.

No sooner did he settle Cormac in the backseat of his police car than he spotted Lily walking briskly in front of Main Street's buildings, headed directly toward him. She had her head down, but—call it twin intuition—he knew she was upset.

"Lil, what's wrong?" He caught her arm as she passed by, and she jerked her head up. She'd been crying. "What happened?"

She brushed her fingers against her cheeks, brown hair that had escaped her braid catching in the moisture left behind. "I'm fine, Joey."

"Uh-huh. You're not. What happened?" And who would he need to set straight?

She raised her chin. "It's nothing I can't handle."

"Stop being stubborn and tell me." He didn't have time for their usual dance.

"Fine." Lily pursed her lips. "I just turned down my third proposal in twenty-four hours."

"Proposal?" He didn't mean to gape quite so much, but *proposals?* "You're not seeing anyone." *Right?*

"You'd think that would matter." Anger sparked in her green eyes. "But no. They think they're 'rescuing' me by making me their wife. They don't care about getting to know me first, let alone anything about my work or the life I've built. I swear, if one more man proposes to me, I might slap him."

Joey caught himself before he rubbed the spot where Katy had slapped him several months ago. "Tell me who it was, and I'll clear things up."

"I already did. You can stand down."

"Lily."

"Joey." But she smiled. Good.

"We'll continue this later. I have a prisoner to transport."

Her brows came up. "Some news doesn't travel as quickly as my marital status. What criminal?"

"You know I can't tell you." He also wished he could suggest she visit with Katy without giving more away than he intended.

"Just be safe, all right? I'm headed back to my barn to get in some target practice before I take the dogs out to the pond."

"You be careful, too, Lil. I don't like all these men paying you unwanted attention. It'd kill me if something happened to you."

She pulled him forward and planted a kiss on his cheek. "Love you, too, brother mine."

Katy stared at the stack of papers the lawyer placed in front of her. Her grandfather had left her money. Not land or an inheritance, per se, but a trust she could draw upon when she became of age.

"I apologize it took me so long to track down the information." The lawyer, a middle-aged man, ran his thumb and forefinger down either side of his graying mustache. "Your hometown is in turmoil right now as it appears the firm that represented your grandfather is under investigation in your uncle's untimely death."

"What?"

"Yes, the body of a Patrick Wells—your uncle, I understand—was found earlier this year, just weeks after one of his lawyers was also discovered dead. Murdered, they now believe. Nasty business."

To put it mildly. What exactly had Fergus Cormac done in a convoluted attempt to marry her?

"It also appears your uncle had been trying to declare you deceased, so that delayed things further. All in all, I managed to have the amount transferred to an American bank. It isn't much, mind you. The financial failures that affected us hit them too."

"How might I go about withdrawing an amount?" Katy clutched the handle of her medical bag. "I need to purchase veterinary supplies."

The man raised his dark brows. "Veterinary supplies?"

"None of the farmers in my town can afford the medicine to save the cows that have been unable to fight their infections. This money will cover it."

"I don't know if that's the best use of the money, my dear. Surely, your grandfather would prefer you use it on something for yourself. A new wardrobe, perhaps?"

Katy was already shaking her head. "Daideó was a veterinarian, like me. He'd be proud of my choice. I'm sure of that."

"Very well." The lawyer reached for a scrap of paper. "Give me the particulars. When you make your purchase, have them send the bill here, and I'll see to it."

After purchasing the medicine, she returned home to gather the rest of her supplies. Anticipation surged through her. Yet she slowed as she passed the mirror over her washstand. She'd worn her veterinarian uniform to show the lawyer she was a businesswoman. Could she loosen her wardrobe now that the threat of her uncle—and being placed in a Magdalene Laundry—didn't hang over her? No. She still struggled to command the respect of the men in Eagle, if Mr. Wallace was any representation. For now, nothing would change outwardly, but inside, she felt freer than she had in her entire life. It gave her hope for the future.

Over the remainder of the day, she injected the cows that weren't responding to her treatment with the new antibiotic, free of charge. It would take several doses to clear the infection, but today was a start. Hope buoyed her as she traveled from farm to farm, seeing to her patients. She spent a bit longer at the Broaders' farm as neighboring farmers helped him bring in his hay. Katy had been paid mainly in eggs, milk, and butter for today's work, and she surreptitiously left as much as she could fit in the Broaders' icebox.

Upon returning home, she hurried to the corral to see her four-legged friends. Nessa and her calf ignored her, as usual, but Glenn stood at the fence, waiting for her. Little remained of Daideó's money now, but she didn't regret spending it on the medicine. The rest she would use to feed Clover, Glenn, and Nessa for the summer if her own hay harvest proved lacking.

Clover worked his way closer to her, hesitant step by hesitant step. He'd barely let her clean his wounds last night and hardly touched his food this morning. Worry tightened Katy's stomach. She slipped into the corral and held a hand out. Clover stopped moving.

Glenn nudged the pocket of Katy's coat. The carrot. She'd forgotten about it last night.

She broke it in half, gave part to Glenn, and the other she held out to Clover. He stepped closer. Closer. Then stretched his neck to take the carrot from her palm.

"That's it, me boy," Katy whispered, bringing her other hand up to rub his nose. "We'll heal you up again, don't you fret."

Clover bobbed his head.

"Right. And we'll take many rides through the fields, just you and me."

Glenn returned to the gate as a car rumbled up the drive. The sound tensed her nerves, but seeing it was Joey's private vehicle, her shoulders eased. Clover trotted to the far side of the corral while she hurried to meet Joey. Gray clouds rolled in overhead. On one hand, they could only hope those clouds would deliver the needed rain so the crops wouldn't die. On the other hand, not too much because with the ground being so dry, a heavy rain would simply wash away the tender plants and potentially destroy the first hay cutting.

"How did things go?" she asked as Joey emerged from his car. The scent of rain laced the breeze that tangled her split skirt about her legs.

"Hello to you too." He smiled, but it didn't reach his eyes.

"What's wrong? Did it not go well? Is there more danger? Did he hurt you?"

Joey caught her hands. "Everything went fine. Cormac won't hurt you again. Tell me about your meeting with the lawyer."

"It is all settled. I used the money to get medicine for the cows." And the threat she'd been running from all her life was gone. She didn't wish Uncle Patrick dead, but the reality was still sinking in. Never again need she fear being sent to a Magdalene laundry.

"Good." But Joey didn't sound like it was good.

She adjusted her fingers in his grasp so that she held his. "Something is wrong. Tell me."

"I don't know what to do about Lily. Found her in tears this morning. When I stopped by Broader's, all I overheard was how every bachelor in the county thinks she's fair game since Amy is getting married. They aren't even planning to ask to call on her. They're just plotting their proposals."

"Oh no."

"Our own mother isn't helping the situation." Joey massaged his forehead. "Why I thought stopping by their house would do anything except give me a headache, I have no idea. Now I don't know what to do." He pressed his palm against her cheek. "How can I be selfish and take her dearest friend away from her when she needs you the most?"

She laid a hand against his chest. "I knew you were a good man, Joey Moore."

"I don't much feel like one when I want to throw everything to the wind and kiss you."

Katy ducked to hide her smile.

"Horsefeathers." Joey pulled her to his chest.

Wrapped there in his arms, his heart beating against her ear, she felt perfectly safe.

He rested his chin on her head. "I'm not sure I can be unselfish, Katy. I'm not sure I'm the good man you think I am."

She pushed away from him, just enough to see his face, startled to see tears shimmering in his eyes. He rubbed his thumb against her jaw, sliding over her lips. Her heart pounded in her chest, but she held herself still. Fear battled with desire. How could she want something and be terrified of it all at once?

He eased her closer and, when she didn't pull away, he dipped his head. In a moment, she was lost in his kiss. The next, she shoved against his chest with a gasp, and he let her go.

Droplets of rain mingled with the tears that dripped down her cheeks. "I'm sorry. I—"

Joey placed a finger on her lips, an arm around her shoulders, his comfort calming her. "You're not ready, Katy."

"I want to be." How she wanted to be.

He wrapped her again in his arms, a cocoon against the gentle rain. She wasn't sure how long they stood there together, but long enough for the sun to peek through the clouds, casting a rainbow in the sky. Katy pointed to it, and Joey shifted enough to face it yet keep her in his arms.

"Amy's wedding." Joey cleared away the emotion that clogged his throat. "Every week, I'll bring you feed for Clover, Glenn, and Nessa. That way, until Amy's wedding, it will give me a proper reason to visit without putting your reputation in question. I care about you, Katy Wells. Deeply. Which is why I'm not going anywhere. I'll be here, waiting, until you're ready, until you feel comfortable taking the next step with me."

"Five months is a long time."

"Not if it leads to forever."

Katy freed her right arm from his embrace so she could rest her hand against his cheek—the cheek she'd slapped months ago when he'd startled her with their first kiss. Joey closed his eyes, leaning into her touch. This would cost him—if only she could save him the hurt, but he was right—she had healing to do before she could give him the full trust he deserved.

With his face turned partly away from her, she slid her hand out of the way to kiss his cheek. "Thank you, Joey Moore."

He pressed his forehead against hers. "Until October."

Then he let her go.

CHAPTER 18

Saturday, October 7

S top fiddling with your tie." Lily adjusted the knot around Joey's neck. He dressed in a suit nearly every day, but for some reason, today's wedding suit felt as though it would choke him. Probably had nothing to do with the warm sun streaming through the windows in his parents' front room.

"If I faint up there, I'm blaming you." He pulled his twin's hands away from his throat and used the opportunity to spin her. "Orange looks good on you."

She stuck out her tongue. "It's peach and you know I hate dresses."

A deep laugh caught him unaware. "What we do for Amy."

"It's a good thing she's our baby sister." Lily rubbed her wrists. "I also dislike no sleeves. And have you seen those gloves I have to wear?"

"The ones that go up to your shoulders?" Maybe a suit wasn't so bad.

"Elbows, but they might as well."

"Oh for heaven's sake." Amy swished into the room looking resplendent in a white gown that sparkled in the sunlight. "The two of you make it sound as though dressing up is akin to torture."

"It is." Joey and Lily spoke at the same time, looked at one another, and laughed.

"Hopeless. Both of you." Amy shook her finger. "You're fortunate I understand. Don't let Mom catch you complaining."

Joey shared a cringing expression with Lily. Their mother would defeather them faster than she could a chicken. Fortunately, Mom was at the church with Dad, assuring herself that everything was set.

"And behave yourselves." Amy raised an eyebrow. "Both of you. You know how hard Andy and I have worked at keeping the peace in this town. With the threat of another statewide strike, we need this to go well. Maybe Eagle will stay out of it this time."

Both Joey and Lily sobered. Joey rubbed the back of his neck, beneath his collar. Lily and Amy didn't even know the half of it. His father supported the strike despite his daughter's wedding. It had caused not a few arguments between Joey and his dad these last few weeks.

"Off with you, now." Amy shooed them through the kitchen. "And be sure Dad is on his way back to get me. Wouldn't want him to get lost, now, would we?"

No, they wouldn't.

Joey drove himself and Lily to the church, leaving Amy at the house alone to wait for their dad to bring her for the ceremony. One thought kept pushing to the forefront of his mind—today was his self-imposed marker for giving Katy the healing space she needed.

The last several months had seen her grow bolder in her care of Eagle's animals. She stayed away from all strike conversation, for which Joey was grateful, but his dad consulted her on the cows' health more frequently than he remembered. However, as far as he knew, she hadn't mentioned any of the summer's events to Lily. At least, Lily hadn't broached any topics regarding her friend, and Joey hadn't volunteered any. His twin had enough on her plate.

"You ready for this?" he asked Lily as he helped her out of the car a block or so from the church.

She wobbled and clutched his arm, frowning at her heeled shoes.

Joey chuckled. "You look nice."

"Nice?" She scrunched her nose. "If even one person suggests I should be married, I might use these heels on them."

He paused before he asked, "Is getting married really that awful?"

"No. It's not that. It's being forced into it because it's everyone's expectation. Then there's not knowing anyone I'd like to spend the rest of my life with. Have you met the men in Eagle?"

There was definite truth to that. "But being single has its lonely side."

"Not with my dogs." She cocked her head, evidence he hadn't disguised the question well enough. "Are you lonely, Joey? You could have your pick of girls in town for a wife."

"Thank goodness you two are here." Mom appeared in front of them, sheathed in an evergreen dress with short, flowing sleeves, a dress so different than her usual, functional cotton ones. She hooked an arm around Lily's and tugged her toward the church, saving him from having to answer the question. "I need you to talk with Andy's friends."

Lily sent an exasperated glance over her shoulder. Joey grinned. He'd keep an eye on whether he needed to rescue her.

He sauntered into the church building, taking in the mums of varying shades that decorated the interior. Mom maintained a tight grip on Lily's arm as they stood before a couple of Andy's friends Joey remembered from school, Alex Chiff and Harry Williams.

The church doors opened, pulling his attention, and Katy entered, pushing every other thought out of his head. She looked gorgeous in a long-sleeved burgundy dress that came to her knees. Heels added a couple inches to her height. Her black hair was gently twisted about her head, with several curls framing her face. Never had he seen her look so … beautiful? It stole his words and left him gaping at her.

"Hi, Joey." She smiled at him.

He got hold of himself and greeted her as he would any friend of the family. Until he could get her alone and ascertain if she was ready to make things more official between them. He refused to damage her reputation by broadcasting to the town that they were together when they weren't. Yet.

"I'll see you afterward." She turned to go into the sanctuary, catching her fingers against his as she did so. A touch that kindled hope.

Joey rubbed the back of his neck. How was he supposed to wait through this entire ceremony before he could talk to her? Even afterward, there'd be too many prying eyes. Because he hoped to finally give her the kiss he'd promised.

Katy stood with Lily against the inside wall of the tent the Moores had set on an open area of their property. She and Lily had helped Mrs. Moore bring out all the food, and now the guests were mingling and congratulating Amy and Andy. She was happy to keep Lily company in this out-of-the-way space. Weddings were overwhelming.

"They look happy." Lily broke the silence between them, not sounding like her usual self.

Katy nodded, waiting for Lily to continue. When she didn't, Katy offered her observation. "You don't appear as happy."

"I'm trying to be." Lily sighed. "One of the ladies called me a disgrace to womankind for not marrying before Amy. Another called me a rebellious suffragist. I supposed I don't mind that title quite so much. It still hurts."

"I'm sorry."

Just as Katy reached to pull her friend into a hug, Mrs. Moore appeared to whisk Lily away, leaving Katy alone. Dare she find Joey? She hoped he hadn't given up on her, that his promise to wait held true, because she'd been counting down to today for a couple weeks now. It wasn't until then that she'd felt ready to pursue more with him, and today she felt even more ready than she did a month ago.

"Dr. Wells?" Mr. Broader approached, pulling his hat from his head.

"How are you?" She gave him her attention, pushing thoughts of Joey aside for now.

"I wanted to tell you personally ... the harvest doesn't look good for us, and the bank has given a final notice. We're selling the property before the bank can take it."

After all the work they'd done, the help from the other farmers, it hadn't been enough?

"I need to find work in the city. Different work." He swallowed hard, and Katy remembered that his farm had been in his family for a couple generations.

"I'm so sorry, Mr. Broader."

"As much as I wish nothing but the best to the newlyweds, their marriage isn't going to solve anything when it comes to dairy prices. I've already told Moore we—they—have to strike again, and mean it. If we don't, I'll simply be another of many farmers forced to leave Eagle."

"Why are you telling me this?"

He looked squarely at her, as if he saw her as an equal. "Farm animals are your livelihood, Dr. Wells, and if the farmers leave, you won't have any patients left. I don't want you to fall on hard times."

Katy pressed a gloved hand to her throat, willing the emotion that rose to go away.

"Might you be in need of chickens?" He looked over his shoulder. "My wife is beside herself that she has to give them up. Knowing they're with you would set her mind at ease."

"Of course. Please tell Mrs. Broader that I'll take right good care of them, don't you worry."

Having lost her desire for celebration, Katy gave her excuses to the bride, groom, and bride's family before returning home. A quick catch of Joey's eye assured her he knew where to find her if he wished.

She changed out of her fancy dress and into her split skirt before calling Clover in from the pasture. A clomping trot brought him to the corral. He greeted her with a whinny, and she smiled. Katy wasn't the only one to need a few months of healing. Clover had too. Together, their spirits had found solid footing.

Clover lowered his head, and Katy wrapped her arms around his neck as far as they'd go. "A ride sounds lovely. What do ya say, boy?"

Clover gave a stuttering hop and nodded his head. Katy laughed. Leading him out of the corral and to the mounting block, she clambered up his back. She didn't ride with reins or a bit anymore, preferring to weave her fingers in his mane. Clover wagged his head, walking in place in his excitement.

As they returned to the corral a bit later, a car rumbled into the drive. Joey's car. She hadn't been long, which meant he hadn't wasted any time coming to visit. Anticipation raced along her limbs. She dropped to the ground and sent Clover into the corral before Joey reached her, still dressed in his fancy suit, though he left the coat in his car.

He stopped beside her, leaning his forearms against the top rail. "How's Clover?"

"Perfect." Katy rubbed the horse's nose and slipped him a treat. "How'd the wedding finish up?"

"Still going on, actually. Lily and I slipped away for a bit."

"How is she? She didn't seem herself." Katy turned so her back faced Clover, who rested his massive head on her shoulder.

"She's always better when she checks on her dogs. And that new puppy of hers needs a lot of attention."

"He's a cute little puppy."

Joey reached for her hand, drawing her closer. "This time was good for you."

He wrapped his other arm around her waist. She tipped her chin to see his face, finding confidence and security there. He waited a breath, and she almost rose up on tiptoes, but he lowered his lips to hers.

Katy lost herself in the kiss. The first one had startled her. The second scared her. This one? She clasped her hands behind Joey's neck. Not a one of the men who'd tried to kiss her—those who thought she was a loose woman because she was born out of wedlock, who assumed because she was an exotic beauty, she was available to them—none made her feel like this.

Before she wanted him to, he pulled away, slowly, leaving light kisses until he held her at arm's length, a tender expression in his eyes. Katy couldn't wipe what she knew had to be a ridiculous grin off her face. She was completely love struck.

"No slap this time." Joey winked.

Katy tugged his vest to bring him down for another kiss.

"Mm, if only all those men who were watching you at the wedding could see this, they'd know you're with me."

"You have no competition, if that's what you're worried about."

"I'd respect your choice, but no, I'm not worried about that. I'm concerned about protecting you. They weren't looking at you as though they had your best interests in mind."

"Like you do." She had no doubts about that, not now.

He straightened, revealing his serious expression. "I know I'll fail miserably at times, but yes, that is my deepest desire. If you'll have me."

"Och, Joey, what can someone like me offer you?"

"Your trust." He ran a finger down her cheek. "And your patience."

"What do you mean?"

"This strike talk … I watched Dad and Booth glaring at one another the entire wedding. Amy is moving into the Booth house until she and Andy know where they'll settle, and Dad is in a fit about it. You know Lily isn't herself. I don't want to bring my family drama into our relationship. Not yet."

"I have no wish to keep secrets, Joey. Not from your family and especially not from Lily."

"Not secrets, just a delayed revelation. A couple days." He closed his eyes and rested his forehead against hers. "I need a place that isn't tainted with turmoil."

"A safe place?'

He nodded.

"Right. Then let's give the wedding excitement a week to settle, then we tell Lily."

"It's a deal." Joey pressed his lips to hers as if imprinting a seal on wax.

"And Joey?" She tilted her head back. "Promise me something else."

"Anything."

"No matter what happens—no matter whether the farmers strike or not, whether money gets tighter, anything at all—that we will always lean on one another and trust each other to work through the troubles to come. I don't want to run away any more."

"Oh Katy. Nothing would make me happier than to make that promise to you." He cupped her cheeks. "I will always stand between you and danger, you and trouble, you and something bad so you never have to run from anything again."

"Seal it?" She tugged him closer.

He grinned. "It'd be my pleasure."

As Joey deepened the kiss, Katy knew this was only the beginning of hope, of a future she could trust, because together, they could face anything.

AUTHOR'S NOTE

The Magdalene Laundries is a horrific stain on Ireland's history. Unfortunately, one that was allowed to continue until the 1990s. Originally a place to rehabilitate fallen women, these workhouses also held those who were orphaned or abused, according to a *New York Times* article entitled, "These Women Survived Ireland's Magdalene Laundries. They're Ready to Talk," written by Ed O'Loughlin (June 6, 2018). Treatment at these facilities was unspeakable, but if you'd like to learn more, I encourage you to look up the *Times* article.

Through the early 1900s, Irish immigrants were often looked down upon in America, but the so-called "Black Irish" even more so. It is unlikely this group of immigrants were of African-American descent. Rather, the term more likely refers to their looks since they usually had black hair, dark eyes, and darker complexions, similar to Katy. However, because they did not look like a traditional Irish immigrant, the term was a derogatory one primarily used in America by non-immigrants and Irish immigrants alike.

According to the history page of the College of Veterinary Medicine at Cornell University, Florence Kimball became the first woman in America to receive a Doctor of Veterinary Medicine in 1910. In fact, seven of the first eleven female DVMs graduated from Cornell. As a nod to this historic opportunity, Katy also received her degree from this prestigious university.

The Wisconsin dairy strikes of 1933 were a culmination of several factors, including low dairy prices, crop-killing drought, and the economic depression affecting the nation (and the world). As portrayed in this story, the first two strikes, in February and May, were increasingly violent with little change brought about. (The report of violence from Joey's chief is from actual events.) Will the farmers in Eagle choose to strike for a third time? Find out in *A Strike to the Heart*, releasing in April 2022 from Heritage Beacon Fiction, an imprint of Iron Stream Media. Then stay tuned for the Christmas novella releasing in September 2022.

Sign up for my Fireside News emails to stay up-to-date on pre-order information for *A Strike to the Heart* and other bookish news. You can use the link bit.ly/FiresideNews or visit my website at daniellegrandinetti.com. I'd love to connect with you on my blog or social media; I'm most active on my bookstagram page, instagram.com/danielleswritingspot. Lastly, if you've enjoyed this novella, I'd be most grateful if you'd take a moment to leave an honest review on your preferred retail site.

Thank you for reading Katy's story. I enjoyed delving into her hidden past while she stood between her patients and their owners as the milk strikes created a tumultuous present. I hope you'll join me for our return to Eagle when Lily must choose whether to trust her family or the man who saves her life.

ACKNOWLEDGEMENTS

It takes many hands to turn an idea into a tangible story for readers to enjoy.

First, I'd like to first thank those at Heritage Beacon Fiction and Iron Stream Media, who will be publishing *A Strike to the Heart* in April 2022, for the permission to dive into the story that came before the novel.

I'd also like to thank my editor, Denise Weimer, for her amazing ability to show me how to make this story shine.

Special thanks to Ann Fryer, not just for reading over the raw form of this story, but for encouraging me in my writing (and personal) life, and helping me through all the details and hurdles of publishing this novella independently.

Another thank you to my sister, Sarah, for double-checking my animal facts. Besides having taken horse-riding lessons for years, she is growing her own small farm. And to Dr. Renée, a horse owner and chiropractor, for filling me in on what it means to own one of those majestic beasts and the companions they might enjoy. All mistakes and liberties are my own.

I'd also like to thank my writing sprinting group for the accountability to keep writing and editing every day. My mother-in-law for proofreading. Alexandra Amor for formatting the e-book. Roseanna M. White for the gorgeous cover and the paperback's interior design.

Lastly, but certainly not least, a great big thank you to my husband

and boys for giving me the time to turn these thoughts into a story for you. And to God, the defender of the weak and protector of the powerless.

ENJOY THIS BOOK?

Continue the series with *A Strike to the Heart,* releasing from Iron Stream Media in April 2022

She's fiercely independent. He's determined to protect her.

Wisconsin, 1933—When a routine mission becomes an ambush that kills his team, Craft Agency sniper Miles Wright determines to find the persons responsible and protect the woman he rescued. But the fierce independence that led Lily Moore to leave her family's dairy business for the solitary life of a dog trainer and the isolation of her farm don't make that easy. Neither does his unwanted attraction to her. Meanwhile, escalating incidents confirm that she's far from safe.

Lily fears letting the surprisingly gentle retired marine into her life almost as much as she fears whoever is threatening her. As Wisconsin farmers edge toward another milk strike, one that will surely turn violent, it becomes clear that the plot against Lily may be part of a much larger conspiracy. When the search for her abductor leads close to home, she must decide whether to trust her family or the man who saved her life.

For details, please visit
daniellegrandinetti.com/a-strike-to-the-heart

Wrap up the series with this Christmas novella
releasing in September 2022.

As Silent as the Night

He can procure anything, except his heart's deepest wish.
She might hold the key, if she's not discovered first.

Chicago, 1933—Lucia Critelli will do anything for her ailing grandfather, including stand in a breadline to have enough food to make him a St. Nicholas Day meal. When she catches the eye of a goon who threatens her grandfather, she discovers the end of Prohibition doesn't mean the end of the mafia's criminal activity.

Retired Marine Scout Giosue "Gio" Vella can find anything, especially if it helps a fellow Italian immigrant, so he has no doubt he can locate his neighbor's granddaughter, who has gone missing from a local church. Keeping her safe is another matter. Especially when he chooses to hide out with his Marine buddy in Eagle, Wisconsin, the site of a barely-held truce among striking dairy farmers.

Will Christmas bring the miracle they all need or will Gio discover there are some things even he can't find, particularly when he stumbles upon the most elusive gift of all: love.

For details, please visit
daniellegrandinetti.com/as-silent-as-the-night

ABOUT THE AUTHOR

Danielle Grandinetti is a book blogger at *DaniellesWritingSpot.com*. Her short stories have appeared in several publications and her writing has won the University of Northwestern Distinguished Faith in Writing Award. Originally from the Chicagoland area, she now lives along Lake Michigan's Wisconsin shoreline with her husband and their two young sons. Danielle especially loves quiet mornings served with the perfect cup of tea.

Made in the USA
Monee, IL
29 December 2021

87531346R00090